Cley

Cley

CAREY HARRISON

HEINEMANN : LONDON

William Heinemann Ltd
Michelin House, 81 Fulham Road, London SW3 6RB
LONDON MELBOURNE AUCKLAND

First published in Great Britain 1991
Copyright © Carey Harrison 1991

A CIP catalogue record for this book
is available from the British Library
ISBN 0 434 31368 8

Printed and bound in Great Britain by
St Edmundsbury Press Ltd
Bury St Edmunds, Suffolk

For Steve, whose tyre tracks led me to Liskeard;
for Simon, for whom *Cley* was written;
and for Sam, my son

Like meaning itself, light does not reside in the scene depicted—it crosses the frame, always from left to right, out of a leaded window so narrowly profiled that we glimpse neither a landscape nor the source of light. In Vermeer the beyond has no features. Yet in our world, in the man-made world of the room illuminated by this transitory light, hangs a map (more precisely the corner of a map) invoking both physical distance and, in its names and contours, the metaphysical distance between knowledge and its object. The human figures, lost in study or in thought, who are interposed between us and the map, share something of its provisional nature, for character is not immanent in Vermeer as it is in Rembrandt, but appetitive, lent by the painter's act and ours. His interiors tell of absent people no less than absent places, conjured in those letters forever to be sent or read once more, to bridge a separation. Those who are present are abstracted, entranced, even asleep. For in essence Vermeer's subjects are always elsewhere: they, and we, are realized by the play of our attention, conjugating reality by a light which is given but whose source is never to be revealed.

—R Lissmann: *Vermeer de Delft, peintre réligieux*,
Auber 1964, translated by John Sarratt

Now I, Joseph, was walking, and I walked not. And I looked up into the air and saw the air in amazement. And I looked up into the heaven and saw it standing still, and the fowls of the heaven without motion. And I looked upon the earth and saw a dish set, and workmen lying by it, and their hands were in the dish: and they that were chewing chewed not, and they that were lifting the food lifted it not, and they that put it to their mouth put it not thereto, but the faces of all of them were looking upwards. And behold, there were sheep being driven and they went not forward but stood still; and the shepherd lifted his hand to smite them with his staff, and the hand remained up. And I looked upon the stream of the river and saw the mouths of the kids upon the water, and they drank not. And of a sudden things moved onwards in their course.

—The Apocrypha: Book of James

I WAS ON BODMIN MOOR, IN A dusty old van parked on the heather, half a mile from the road. Through the windscreen I could see the Hurlers, a low circle of standing stones beneath a gentle tumulus. And all around, the gold of the gorse. The van was hot and musty but I stayed inside it. It smelt of holidays taken in it when I was a child, in this van and my mother's previous one. It smelt of her.

I'd been hunting for my mother all weekend. She lived in London, in the basement of a tall, forbidding house in Highgate, on a wide street lined with mournful trees. Geoffrey, the landlord, said she'd gone to Cornwall. For a week or two, he said. In the van. This was common practice; in the summer she preferred to live in the van, and often set off without warning. But a week or so could turn into a month, and I needed to find her right away. *Where* in Cornwall? 'Bodmin?' Geoffrey had dithered, in his usual distracted way, 'no, not Bodmin: Liskeard.' Liss-card, he'd pronounced it; on the map it beckoned with an odd, intrusive 'e'. I set out after work on Friday, in the car, trusting to luck and a kind of homing instinct—a matter of putting myself in Mother's place, really, while I searched. I enjoyed this. On the other hand, my fortnight's holiday was just beginning and I didn't want to spend it all on Mother's trail.

I'd taken a big decision, the biggest of my life to date, and I simply wanted to tell someone—or rather, because there were plenty of people I could tell, I wanted the moment of decision (as being more important, in a sense, than the wedding ceremony that might follow it) properly witnessed, *solemnized* as the old church banns say; but I couldn't think whom to go to for this, so it was Mother I went looking for, Mother who was the last person to get excited about the prospect of a marriage. So much the better. Her blessing would be worth winning.

The journey down was a disaster. I'd hoped to start it in mid-afternoon, leaving the bookshop in a fellow-assistant's care, but she failed to return from lunch and finally showed up at five, alleging an adventure. The bookshop where I work is in King Street, just off Hammersmith Broadway, and an hour earlier I would have reached the motorway ahead of the weekend traffic. Instead I got stuck in it. By the time I reached Bristol it was drizzling, and with the winding roads to come I realized I wouldn't be in Liskeard much before midnight. I'd already found and phoned a hotel there, during the week, so I rang them from the Knight Of The Road café: they promised there would be someone on the door till two a.m.. I drove on, reassured. Soon after, I took pity on two hitchhikers standing at the roadside in the spitting rain. Going to Cornwall, they said, to Land's End. They were a year or two younger than I was—I'd turned twenty-three in June—a boy and a girl, very quiet, with a tent. I discovered that they were returning from some kind of religious festival in Germany: their holy man was on a flying visit from the East. In the last few months I'd become rather interested in Sufism, and I tried to find out whether we had any beliefs in common. But these two were either indifferent to Islamic mysticism or else their own beliefs were inarticulate, because I couldn't get much out of them, only that they'd learnt to create, spontaneously, the taste of nectar in their mouths. They wouldn't tell me how.

The more I questioned them the slower I drove, and I began to get anxious about my two a.m. deadline. I gave up on conversation, and we went up onto the bumpy Dartmoor roads at a terrific clip, despite a rising mist. The couple behind me were completely silent. Then one of them, the boy, was sick. Luckily he warned me early; we stopped, and he staggered out onto the grass, watched by the sheep. Now was the time, I suggested when he came back, to create the taste of nectar. He said he was working on it. We went on, more cautiously, stopping at intervals for the boy to be sick. Princetown prison, eerily lit by its searchlights, was on the horizon when he stopped me for the fourth time; mercifully they decided to pitch their tent there for the night, in a deserted sheepfold. It was twenty-five past one when I roared off. But the worst was yet to come. No sooner was I off the moor and out of the mist than a car came straight out of a side road at me, from the left. I was going too fast to brake in time. He barely braked at all, hit me hard in the rear of the car, and raced on across the junction. I skidded to a halt; but he was gone, I was late, and the car was still in running order. I drove on.

Its name blazoned in letters four feet high, my hotel dominated the main and, as it turned out, Liskeard's only square. I took a quick look at the car and the crumpled rear wing, and hurried to the granite portico of the hotel. There was a light, and an old man who led me up a monumental staircase. My room had once been a magnificent apartment, now divided into narrow cubicles. The ceiling was fifteen feet above the bed. Briefly and ludicrously crossing it, over the window, was a huge portion of moulding, silhouetted at intervals by the glow from a neon sign across the road. I slept poorly, worrying about the car, the crash—it had felt like a kick up the backside in return for my impatience with the holy hitchhikers—and the coming search for my mother. All night, it seemed, cars trundled through Liskeard towards the coast, keeping me awake, cars with trailers, boats, and caravans; at one point a small collision got me out of bed to look, vindictively pleased, and glad that I wasn't the only collision victim that night. I watched the drivers, one of whom had shattered a headlamp, trying to determine the extent of the damage by the faint light of the Empire Fruit Shop. Their only other aid was the flickering café sign that lit my ceiling, a neon fish whose mood evoked my own, a fellow-insomniac in whose blue-ringed belly 'And Chips' flashed on and off like a case of indigestion.

The search for Mother followed a time-honoured procedure. First, after breakfast, a leisurely drive around the town and the outskirts, looking for a pale blue van. Next, visits to the garages, the newsagents, and the hardware stores, those selling Camping Gaz to fuel Mother's cooker. At lunchtime, round the pubs. I drew a blank. But it was a sunny day, and I saw Liskeard. I found it a peculiar place. It had few charms, and fewer tourists. It was full of signs to other places, as though by way of apology; it was on the route to everywhere else, and no-one stopped in it—motorists filed through, reading the signs. To Looe, to Bodmin, to Plymouth, to Tavistock. Cars crawled patiently down the Parade, past a conventional line of High Street shops. A wedding appeared to be taking place in Lloyd's Bank; the bride and her family blocked the doorway. I looked up and saw *Solicitor* inscribed on the first floor windows, with more guests visible inside. Below, the bride stepped out onto the pavement and brought a newly lit cigarette to her lips. The cars had stopped; I watched her. She took a long drag, dropped the cigarette, and crushed it quickly and brutally underfoot. Then she turned back into the doorway and vanished upstairs with her relatives. The traffic jolted forwards.

But this busy street, I found, was only a front, an illusion of normality. Liskeard was built like an inverted cone: around the rim, the shops, the wedding, and the circling cars, with gulls wheeling and cackling overhead as though at what they alone could see—the old centre of the town, in the dip, with steep lanes running down to it. This was virtually deserted, crumbling, boarded up, with roofless

6

houses and walls sprouting blackberries and buddleia. Metal advertisements, some of them upside down, praised defunct products. The old well remained, with water which never ran dry, according to a plaque above it, and could still be relied upon for 'beneficial effects on matrimony'. The water looked filthy. Farther on I found a scrap merchant, and an occult bookshop called Original Hollow. There, in the middle of Saturday afternoon, I traced my mother.

She had bought several pamphlets from them, on the local sights of supernatural interest, and had enquired after a sinister tor on the moor, near the town of Minions, where Aleister Crowley was supposed to have conducted black masses. I turned down the offer of a Chinese horoscope and climbed back up to the rim, the living town, where a trail of multicoloured confetti littered the pavement and led me back to the hotel.

Sinister tors, hauntings: I'd never had any special sympathy with this preoccupation of my mother's. It had taken me, during my childhood, to some interesting places. Dark, windy hills, with a thermos of coffee at our side. Disgruntled farmers came for us, but nothing more other-worldly. I had yet to be convinced.

It was half past three or so when I approached the moor; the fields gave way abruptly, as before a sea. Even on a sunny day it was a sombre sight, the ruins of the tin mines overgrown with creepers, the granite reefs peeping from the bracken and the gorse. A dead sea, a drained sea casting up its dead, the chimneystacks and ruined enginehouses dotting the horizon like wrecks. I drove through tidy retirement hamlets lined with polite hydrangeas, and up onto the high plateau of Craddock Moor, towards Minions. The blue van was instantly visible, beached on the heather. Beside it rose a tall stack flanked by flying buttresses, looking like a space-rocket in one of my childhood comics. I parked by the road; I didn't want Mother to see the gash in the car, which by daylight was as bad as I had feared.

When I reached it, the van was empty. In the back, the mattress and the sleeping bag, the clothes, and the books, all damp from nighttime vigils, filled it with familiar smells. Dear, hateful smells; they brought back old silences, old stalemates, hours of sulking on the road with neither of us prepared to break the deadlock; an only child playing husband to a widowed mother, both of us hooked on it. It was the same now, I couldn't get out of the van. On the bench seat lay the pamphlets from Original Hollow, *A Miner's Fancies* by Commander the Honourable R H Kitto, *Llys Kared of the Holy Grail* by a doctor from Darite, *Feasts and Folklore, Cornish Superstitions*. I took them and walked to the rocketship, and read them in the shade. The old miners had seen imps and demons underground, and white rabbits that vanished down the wind bore. I gazed round, over the gorse blossom. No sign of Mother's short, firm figure. The moor stretched out before me, gilded, featureless. Grassy paths meandered round and through the gorse, serene, with miniature pyramids of granite thrusting upwards through the grass like the tips of buried obelisks, twinkling with mica; a stained-glass window landscape, a stylized Golgotha. Here, surely, was the time and place for a visitation. But none came, no virgin queen, no hooded monk, nothing from Mother's crowded anthologies. All the same, the empty landscape and the ivy-covered enginehouses testified to more than fallen industry. I knew something of Cornish history, for my father's family came from Padstow, north of the moors, and my grandfather had left a collection of solemn, edifying books on the subject, shorn of imps and demons but still enthralling. A history of secret survival.

From where I was sitting, on a granite windowledge, I could see one of the mineshafts, its mouth surrounded by a cautionary wire fence. Heather had grown around it, garlanding the hole, a doorway, cheerful and enticing, as though the real Cornwall began here, underground. A few miles east, on Hingston Down, the Cornish Church had made a final, armed stand. Last of the Celtic churches to submit to Rome, its followers died on the battlefield for their saints, their calendar, and their distinctive flowing tonsure. It was then that they went underground, they, their religion, and succeeding generations of Cornishmen working deep beneath those Downs, dying there in their thousands, in their tens of thousands, by rockfall, by fire, by flood. Ruined, the enginehouses now stood revealed as penitential cloisters: there was no mistaking the design, in silhouette, with the machinery removed. Against the sky, the shallow arches of the windows and the great stone portals declared themselves true to the old religion. As dusk came on I walked back to the van. Still empty. I lay down on the mattress in the back, and slept.

Something was sniffing at my feet. I jerked upright. It was pitch dark; there was a scuffling noise. A head appeared. It was the dog.

'Mother?' I called.

'Who's that?' Her voice was muffled.

'It's me. It's Jack.'

'Where are you?'

She sounded quite unnerved. I poked my head out of the back, and a torch shone on my face. Mother chortled in the darkness.

'It is you.' The torchlight left my face, and I heard her go and open the sliding door at the front of the van. 'Hup... hup!' The dog, an irritable Scottie, scrambled in, and the door slid shut.

Mother came round to the back, her stocky frame now visible as she put down the torch. She seemed to be wearing more pullovers than usual. 'What is it?' she said. 'What's happened?'

'Nothing. I wanted to talk to you.'

She dragged some matches from her cardigan pocket and started to light a gas lamp, beside me. 'I've been to Siblyback, where Crowley made his sacrifices.'

'What was it like?'

'The wretched dog wouldn't come up the path. Ran off howling.' She didn't bother to glance at me for effect; she knew I wouldn't be impressed. The gas lamp flamed, and Mother's chubby face hovered over the hissing globe, disembodied: 'Well?' I had to look away, under her gaze.

The image of Liskeard's wishing well returned, full of débris, cigarette butts. Confetti in the High Street. 'I think I'm going to marry Chrissie.'

'Oh Christ,' she said, and chuckled again. 'That's funny. And I dreamt you were dead, the other night.'

MY NAME IS Wilfred Denis Thurgo, or so my passport says, Wilfred after my mother's father, a clergyman, deceased; Denis after a wartime chum of my father's, also long since dead. When I was kicking in my mother's womb, Father called me Jumping Jack, and the name—I'm glad to say—outlasted my christening. Richard, my papa, was a solicitor, very respectable, not especially well off, with a compulsion to defend the destitute and a penchant for silly jokes. He taught me, I gather, that the moon is not a heavenly body but a piece of cardboard suspended over New Barnet; and died before I was old enough to query this. (I don't actually remember him saying it, or, since my images of him derive from snapshots, saying anything.) Absent fathers, as it happens, run in the family: my grandfather died in the Great War shortly after my father was born, and my grandmother, who disliked her son even as a baby, handed him over to her own father, an Irish engineer who ignored the child in favour of his lifelong obsession, a plan to raise Armada galleons from the depths of Galway Bay.

In my case, the disappearing act took place as follows. One fine spring day Father received the news that a paternal uncle had died at his retirement home in Spain, leaving some of his effects to his favourite nephew. The legacy consisted of books and clothes, some war mementoes—the late uncle had liked to be known as 'the Colonel'—and an old jeep. Father flew to Malaga and, three days later, vanished without trace. He had taken the Colonel's jeep out for a spin, which was puzzling in itself, and ominous, since Father had never learnt to drive. Nothing more had been heard, of man or machine. Molly—my mother—went out to Spain at once. She returned without news. Finally, after hellish months, the Malaga police phoned. A goatherd had found the burnt-out jeep and Father's body, in a ravine, hidden from roadside view. Mother travelled to Spain once more, identified the body and made arrangements to have Papa shipped home for burial, amid the appropriate ceremony, in Highgate cemetery; she didn't feel that the crash, and the horror of the ensuing fire, would have done anything to alter Richard's hatred of cremation. It was over. I grew up without a father; and it wasn't till many years later that I learnt some of the odder details surrounding his death.

Out of delicacy, perhaps, the Spanish police hadn't told Mother the full extent of her husband's burns. It was a shock when the sheet was pulled back, in the Malaga morgue, to reveal a corpse unrecognisably charred except for two large and oppressively pink feet on the end of it, in front of her. Blistered by the heat but otherwise unharmed, they'd been protected by the Colonel's old army boots. The chief of police raised his eyebrows at Mother; Mother nodded; the feet slid back into refrigeration, and Mother emerged into the spring sunshine, to wander along the Malaga seafront in a daze. The scene in the morgue had left its mark on her. Now, on the beach, there were feet everywhere she looked. She began to study them. They were the same, they were different, some were funny, some were just feet. But would she have recognized her husband's, without hesitation, if they had come padding towards her?

The relief she'd felt, when the news came that Richard's body had been found, was too precious to abandon and Molly held onto it now, letting it carry her through the funeral arrangements. She didn't tell anyone just how reduced were the remains in the coffin they buried. It seemed unhelpful for people round a grave to know that they were crying over feet. But feet were all there was, and there remained, inevitably, a nagging doubt in Mother's mind. In the end she had, as she later admitted to me, hired a man to make his own investigation of the death. Nothing came of it. The only other person missing at the time, from nearby Malaga, was a German tourist, and although neither the local police nor those in the tourist's home town had yet resolved the mystery of Herr Schäfer's disappearance, they didn't seem greatly concerned. He was an underworld figure, a black-marketeer, so the story ran, who had slipped off to Spain with the collective loot, and his 'friends' were confidently believed to have caught up with him. There the trail went cold, to everyone's relief. And Richard—or rather his feet—lay quiet in the grave.

The investigation ate into the meagre funds Father had left, and I owe my continued education, at the privileged level at which it had begun, to my mother and a fever of home knitting, which she performed for the advertising and display departments of a London woollens manufacturer. Even after I won the first of several scholarships, she continued to fill the world with pullovers, well beyond the call of duty, on what appeared to be a zither strung with metal bedsprings. But at one point, when I was barely twelve, it became clear to Mother that we didn't have enough to pay the coming school fees, and eat. She took herself and our last hundred pounds to Sandown Park, one summer afternoon. She had never placed a bet in her life. What followed—the day, the choice of horse, the race itself—is too good a story not to have become grossly distorted over the years, in the family annals; but what is certain is that Mother put it all on one horse at 40-1, and it won. The horse's name was Second Sight.

We paid the bills; and that year, at school, I discovered mathematics—or rather it discovered me, one term when our regular maths master was ill and a man called Bromley, 'Bomber' Bromley, substituted for him—and it was to carry me through my remaining education without further recourse to Sandown Park. It was also about this time that my mother's interest in the occult began to manifest itself. It didn't seem to bear directly on the faint aura of mystery surrounding father's death: to my knowledge Mother never consulted mediums. She liked to go directly to the epicentre of occult experience, to explore it herself, preferably out of doors. I encouraged her. It took us out of Highgate, and away from pull-overs.

At twelve I found multiple equations ridiculously easy; and I wanted to please 'Bomber' Bromley, who was useless at maths but who picked the school cricket team. Numbers stick, I found, they've got nowhere to run to—at least until you're sixteen, or eighteen, when they warned us that for most the inspirational period was over, clouded by worldly matters or perhaps simply by words. All the same my knack for sums got me to university, thank goodness, because there I met Chrissie in my first and as it turned out only year. As a mathematician I was certainly flagging; I told my mother, darkly, that I was more interested in questions that didn't have answers. I was even more interested in Chrissie, who was small and dark and Jewish, and clever, and gentle. At home she was Christina, an unlikely name for a Jewish child, but her parents only looked bemused when I pointed this out, as though they hadn't noticed the anomaly. She was an English student, and with her I began to read. Until then, music had been my main, my only outlet. Records got me through my last two years at school. Miles Davis, Gerry Mulligan; I knew Chet Baker's solos note for note. Books were a broadening; Chrissie and I were argumentative. I was cocksure, in our discussions, no doubt because I felt I had a life outside the university, in a real, hard-headed, professional world: in a band. At school some friends and I had formed The Fallen Angels; we played in straw boaters, at dances in the Home Counties. None of the other Angels found a place at university, and at the end of that first year I faced a choice. The band was going strong, we'd cut a record which, bizarrely, was a hit in Yugoslavia; we had a manager and autumn dates in the south of France. University seemed tame, compared to rock and roll. The choice was obvious.

We flopped. It was we who were too tame, too genteel. The new bands were smashing guitars on stage. We played 'Blue Moon' and 'Jezebel'. The great divide between the earlier and later Sixties opened at our feet; old friendships fell into the chasm; we lost our best musician to a rival group, amid recriminations, struggled on for a year and then went our separate ways. I got a job, briefly, doing the band arrangements for a musical about Americans in Europe, full of bright young English actors. It too flopped. I was at my lowest ebb. It was June, and Chrissie was taking her final exams. I knew I was no better than a journeyman musician: the numbers stuck, they didn't run. Perhaps no-one would notice, with the onset of a new musical barbarity. But I was no barbarian, I was—as Chrissie told her parents—a serious boy. And literature, with Chrissie as my guide, had opened other vistas. I had a brand-new urge: to be of use.

Chrissie began teaching, at a primary school; she was useful if poorly paid. Each summer she went off to Italy as a courier, shepherding tourists round the monuments. We were happy then and unthreatened. We trusted one another. Her family, German by extraction, took me to their ample bosom, and were a revelation to me: such a plenitude of aunts and uncles. Fathers too, and grand-fathers. It fostered the Englishman's ready contempt for his own dislocated family existence. This attitude, in turn, they loved—it justified their ways. They had nothing but daughters: I came to them, a son, out of the wilderness of hard hearts. A disciple. Fired by my new altruism I went to work in Aldgate, at a self-styled social workshop. They needed people, even inexperienced ones—this was before the days when social science graduates were two a penny; there were plenty of better jobs going, and eager beavers were in short supply.

I arranged sing-songs for the old folks, and played the piano. In the evenings I taught English to Pakistanis, many of them elderly. Dirty good deeds, as my mother put it. Each evening I returned, numb, to the flat I shared with Chrissie. We were both too tired to talk. And when a new broom, in the form of a new warden, came to Aldgate, re-allocating funds to more professional quarters, I was only too relieved to find that I was fired. I found a new job with a Church adoption society, mostly doing the paperwork, occasionally visiting their transit homes, where harassed administrators struggled to keep oversexed teenagers under lock and key. My reforming zeal was on the wane. I had begun to dream of travelling again. America. I wanted to see it, to hear it, to sit, perhaps, at Gerry Mulligan's feet, beneath his mighty baritone: the jazz critic. I foresaw a West Coast life, began to save money towards it. It never occurred to me that I was threatening my relationship with Chrissie, but I didn't picture her in San Francisco. And in those days we never spoke of marriage, Chrissie and I. It was first love. Not strictly the first, for Chrissie; but it was for me. I was proud of it, proud to have developed a first love into a friendship, a routine, a kind of imitation marriage. There didn't seem anything callous about leaving for America; Chrissie was my girlfriend; and we never spoke of babies.

But then came the bookshop in Hammersmith, and I stayed—it was too good an opportunity to ignore. The place had started as a music shop, it was an old haunt of mine, specializing in American imports. The little ground floor premises began to expand into the upper floors; the owner, Sue Harding, bought a house around the corner and opened a bookshop, importing paperbacks and magazines. Sue came from the States herself, from Charlottesville, Virginia. There were great plans for King Street in our minds: street theatre, music, advisory bureaus, neighbourhood politics, a community centre. It was 1968. Sue had money. I was to run the bookshop; I was twenty-three years old and I had everything I wanted. Including Chrissie.

The problem was that there was no problem, only an increasing illusion of adulthood and a sense that I had got there too fast. The bookshop prospered, I had a steady income, and I could afford to help my mother out financially; to give her treats. With her growing eccentricity, and my solid citizenship, I often felt that I was the parent, prematurely middle-aged, and she the child. But we were fast friends. The crisis over Chrissie, on the other hand, was gathering, but it was gathering entirely in my own mind. We had been together five years: I was possessed with the idea that I ought to marry her, that I ought to do something, that I ought to decide. She and I had by this time discussed and dismissed marriage, pending a desire for babies, or more exactly an appropriate plateau in Chrissie's career. We agreed, as usual. Our chief disharmony was social, as it were, rather than intellectual, or sexual. My friends aggravated her, and she them. Musicians, would-be communards, occasional lecturers—she called them stargazers, woolgatherers, and used her mother's phrase, *kein Stehvermögen*: no stamina. I agreed with her. That was what I liked about them, they were uncommitted. I saw them on my own, increasingly, leaving Chrissie to her pupils' homework.

Our sexual history was, I thought, rather encouraging. For the first few years all the climactic satisfaction was my own; the night Chrissie announced her first orgasm I was so proud I nearly proposed then and there. It soon became a familiar accomplishment, though Chrissie was very particular about the time and place for making love: the 'mood'. She was romantic, as she chose to put it, often to my frustration. Later, watching people's marriages wither in the face of physical boredom, I felt this rationing had its merits. I wasn't bored with her, or she with me. I hadn't been unfaithful, no, not once; I was a serious boy. I just wanted to know what else there was to life. First love; Blue Moon; or just a cardboard one, over New Barnet?

There was no moon at all that night, on Bodmin Moor, and I

16

stumbled frequently in the bracken, on the way back to my damaged car. Mother had kept the torch to light her return to Siblyback, this time without the superstitious dog. I could see the faint beam in the distance as she forged into the dark. She knew what she wanted. And as usual our conversation had been short but sweet.

'Has Chrissie found somebody else?'

'No.' I stared at her. 'Not as far as I know.'

'I see,' she said, and mused. 'Funny. I rather thought that you wanted to break it up.'

'No, not at all. I want to marry her.'

'I see.' We sat in silence. 'Well, I'm not going to advise you, you know. Is it advice you want?'

'Yes.'

'Well,' she paused, 'if you don't know now, you'll never know, will you?'

'Precisely,' I said. But I wasn't quite sure we meant the same thing. In the ensuing silence Mother gathered herself up, folded a blanket and put it underneath her arm.

'Come and meet Crowley,' she said. 'You won't regret it.'

'Did *he* believe in marriage?'

She ignored this. 'I've got to move on tomorrow, and I don't want to lose this one. I only came back to park the dog. Well? Are you coming or aren't you?'

'Sorry, I think I'm going to cry off,' I made a time-honoured excuse, 'on grounds of fatigue.'

'On grounds of coffee, eh?' This too was time-honoured, a Goon Show leftover. The truth was, I didn't really want to discuss my future over Crowley's ghost. We agreed to meet for lunch next day, at the hotel, and 'thrash it out properly'. To the sound of the Scottie barking furiously in the locked van, we made our separate ways.

I drove back to the sturdy cube of the hotel. In the bar I made conversation with the owner, a tall, dark-haired woman in her forties.

She seemed depressed. 'When the bypass comes,' she said gloomily, 'we'll up sticks.' I spoke admiringly of the oak panelling, the staircase, and the granite front. 'Used to be three of them,' she said, 'The Red Lion in Bodmin, that's a supermarket now, and the one in Truro.' I asked about the one in Truro. 'Demolished. The brakes failed on an articulated lorry—I *don't* think. It came straight down the hill and drove into the foyer. Just what the planners wanted.'

The owner's daughters, both rather attractive, lounged at the far end of the bar, on seats of orange leatherette. But I sat quietly over my drink; what this planner wanted was a chaste, contemplative summer alone. Mentally I rehearsed my speech about the paradox of freedom through security, in marriage, for the morrow. Freedom through security. What did I mean? Freedom from anxiety perhaps. One thing I knew: my mother wouldn't tax me with my past, or her past, or my father's past. She never did. Past was taboo.

In the event, the lunch went by without a single mention of the marriage or of Chrissie. We talked of everything and everybody else. Mother never raised the subject; nor did I; and as the meal progressed it seemed to me that this was what I'd come for, what I wanted. To know that I didn't need advice.

After coffee, we strolled out to the van. The sun shone down on an empty Parade.

'What's Chrissie think?' she said abruptly.

'She doesn't know yet, I was going to write to her. She's still in Florence, shepherding the tourists.' Mother gave me a long look. 'Well,' I said, 'it's good money, you know.' She was still looking sceptical; I grinned. 'Chrissie likes it. Gets her away from me.'

'You'd better make your mind up,' Mother said. 'I had to ask your father, you know.' She leaned into me, small but belligerent, a teasing bullock. 'Twice.'

THAT SUMMER THE sun shone as if for ever. It was shining at

seven in the morning as I wrestled with my bicycle outside Mother's basement flat, and dragged it up onto the pavement. I kept it in Highgate; there wasn't room in Hammersmith, in the flat. I pedalled gently down the tree-lined street. Before me lay a journey of a hundred miles and more.

I wore my tried and tested cycling clothes: shorts, a baggy shirt, a jacket, on my head a Peugeot cycling cap. The saddle and the old tape on the handlebars felt comfortable and familiar. I rode slowly through the North Circular traffic, out of London, out into the Essex countryside. My destination was a place called Cley, on the Norfolk coast, Cley-next-the-Sea, where Sue Harding owned a cottage. Sue was my employer; our friendship dated from the ill-fated show featuring my band arrangements and Sue herself, in the part of an American heiress. Which in reality she was. The family money was in wool, a material I knew well; it was even possible that I owed my start in life to Sue, via Mother's knitting, though Sue's woollen mills were not in her native Virginia, but in Germany, home of her ancestors. Sue herself, and her husband David, had made an enormous impact on me when I met them. They were fifteen years older (in David's case a few years more) than I was, they were the married couple, worldly-wise. They cooked exotically and competitively; they were raunchy and combative, they flirted and feuded with each other with mysterious gusto; it all struck me as natural and fine and unattainable. I couldn't wait to tell Sue I was going to marry Chrissie. I knew I'd get a better reception from her, a loving and considered and above all a celebratory one. That was the blessing I wanted: I would be treated like an adult whether a foolish one or not. Mercifully, I could find in myself no trace of desire for Sue, lovely as she was. There was a bovine something in her eyes, in her face generally a large placidity meant for mothering, or so it seemed to me. I had certainly tried to picture her younger and friskier, but to no avail, an untamed Sue was no more to be imagined than a schoolboy David. In their London apartment I spent trailing afternoons watching the famous come and go, listening to stories of beatniks and Birdland. Sue was a singer first and foremost. Ramblin' Jack Elliot would be crashed out on the sofa in his boots, the silver Ferrari double-parked outside the door. Fitzroy from Kingston, the Jamaica Kingston, was rapping in the hall. I hung around; drank tea—bourbon when David was there—played records, and waited for David. He was often away abroad at conferences with titles pertaining to dreams or ancient magic, and on his return would retreat to East Anglia, to write and ruminate, to farm, and to edit *The Whale*, an occasional, omnivorous journal whose themes were poetry, psychology, and myth. Sometimes I was allowed to visit him in the country, more often not, when David was writing; but he might come to town at any time. And Sue was always there, at home, in town. It was she who drew the famous, the musicians, to their flat, she too who brewed the tea, who made the neighbours welcome and invested in local causes; but she was shedding her American ways, becoming Anglicized; and it was David who drew me. Idaho-born, tall, barrel-chested, balding, he would drive out undesired friends of Sue's by sticking a corncob pipe in his mouth and playing Ezra Pound. The yellow pipe suited his cherubic, bearded face rather well, better than the 'ol' Ezry' bark. His training was in philosophy and literature but now he was into pigs, real, grunting, black and white pigs, rare pigs, which he kept on a farm in Suffolk. There he sought the final silence and compulsion of the animals. In London, however, he talked. He talked a lot about The Metaphor; likened his own speech to a 'cubist potage'; taught me about antinomianism, Nietzsche, and the pig, about Hegel and Charlie Marx, about Faust and Mephisto and the meaning of animal husbandry in the 'late Twentieth'. He carried a Bible, proclaiming 'And thou shalt be an husbandman!' But the pig farm failed. It was a bad time for the pigmeat industry; one of David's Suffolk neighbours hanged himself in his own piggery, on Christmas Day.

Wool never failed. Sue and David sold the farm, and bought the little house in Cley, keeping the London salon for the winter months. Sue was singing Allegheny Mountain songs, with her zither—no bedsprings on this one—to folk club audiences. She had given up the stage. David was searching for an academic post, he had applied to somewhere in America; this was the last I'd heard. On my return from Liskeard and my mother, I found a letter waiting.

Jackson potato, it ran, *August heeby-jeebs in Norfolk. Why is the damn place so still? (I don't scare easy you motherfuckahs—come out of the shadows!) So I am taking a plane back to Chicago to see if the professors think my teeth are still fit for the institutional tit. If you are solo come to Cley to comfort my abandoned ladies. But take it easy, the ladies have had all they can take of the shaky burger libido, not perhaps part of my charm, but part of my esse. And yours, Jackson.*

I was a little puzzled by the plural ladies but I took it this included Sue's daughter Stefanie, now aged ten or eleven, the fruit of Sue's first, Virginian, marriage. David's letter continued in this vein over the page, apologizing for the 'disintegrative syntax,' and hinting darkly at some domestic upset. But he ended: *Don't get me wrong. We have been CIVIL. Byron without tears.* In the margin he had scribbled, *that's quite good, what?* Finally, *Whether this means we are all decorously avoiding a big communal deposit of infantile faeces in the front hall is a text I leave you to construe for me when I return from the home of the brave and the land of the freeway. Salud. D.*

It was a lovely day for a cycle ride. I wasn't fit, but the first day usually isn't too bad. I kept my mind off the discomfort by calculating my mean average speed. Ardleigh reservoir gleamed in the sun, East Bergholt snuggled in the trees; outside Marks Tey a herd of goats looked up to watch me pass. David's words came back to me from time to time. His peculiar voice made it hard to tell despair from jocularity, but I saw no cause for alarm: his was a marriage that could absorb, I was certain of this, a good deal of buffeting. I reached Ipswich for lunch, on schedule, ate a gammon steak and chips, drank lager, and proceeded shakily. It was too hot. I left the dual carriageway at Needham Market and passed out under a hedge, drunk on sun.

It was late, but still light, when I freewheeled into Cley, flushed and triumphant. One hundred and forty-seven miles in just over ten hours' riding. A woman with a London voice gave me directions to the cottage, on a green outside the village.

Newgate Green was wide and well-tended, and dominated by a huge, incongruously splendid church. There were a handful of new bungalows. Sue's cottage was a pretty flint affair, with clematis in bloom around the door. The lights were on upstairs. I knocked. My legs felt newly sewn on. A girl with long blonde hair opened the door; it wasn't Sue.

'Hello,' I said.

'You're Jack.'

'I'm Jack.'

She was pretty, I felt acutely bedraggled, and took off my Peugeot cap.

'Sue's gone to fetch Stefanie. We thought you weren't coming.'

I asked where I could put the bike. Her eyes widened. 'You cycled all the way?'

'My car wasn't ready,' I said modestly. 'Someone ran into it last week.'

We took the bike round the side of the cottage, in the shadow of the church. The girl, on closer inspection, couldn't be more than eighteen or nineteen. She seemed to know her way. In profile she was prettier still. Byron without tears. Who was she?

I propped up the bike in the back garden. As the girl led me into the house through the kitchen door, I noticed paint marks, multicoloured, on her hands.

'You're in the middle of something,' I said.

'No no,' she said. 'Would you like a drink, or what? You must

22

be famished, too. I'll cook you something.'

I took the drink first. This was a mistake. Before it hit me, I wandered round the pleasant sitting room. Musical instruments, books, paintings. One in particular caught my attention. It was small, and modern, and representational, painted in loving photographic detail. It was a street scene, viewed through an exaggeratedly tall doorway, as tall as it might seem to a child. Out of the doorway, and partly obscured by it, a man was leading a boy and another child, sex indeterminate, in shadow. On the far pavement, an elderly female figure was escaping, bisected by the edge of the picture. At an upper window of the house opposite, another figure, sex similarly indeterminate, stood watching.

'Yours?' I tried, nodding at the painting as the girl came in, bringing me fried eggs.

'No,' she said. 'It's French.'

I thanked her for the eggs, and sat down. 'Look,' I said, 'I'm afraid I don't know who you are.'

'Of course you don't,' she said, and laughed. 'I'm sorry, I'm Claire. I'm the nanny. Well, I'm a friend of Sue's really.'

I nodded. She had a sweet and wary look; was that how nannies looked? My head was beginning to swim, with the ride and the Scotch. I felt terrible.

'I'm in disgrace, actually,' she went on. 'As a nanny.'

'Oh?'

'I let Steffie run across the road, in Sheringham. She's always doing it. Are you all right?'

I struggled with my fried eggs in a mist. At some point, Sue arrived, with a warm, beautiful smile on her face. She was pushing Stefanie towards me. 'You remember Jack,' she said. 'No,' said the child. I grinned foolishly, and the women put me to bed in David's study.

Photographs of my mentor in his younger days stared at me from the walls. Beardless David standing before a mountain of rusting cars, with somebody who looked like Kerouac. David in a canoe. David escorting Jackie Kennedy. No it wasn't. It was Kennedy escorting Jackie Kennedy. I thought again of the delicious Claire; nanny my Irish aspidistra. I passed out again and slept till eleven the next morning.

SUNLIGHT FILLED THE room. With aching limbs I levered myself out of bed and went to the window. Beneath me spread the little back garden, attractively unkempt, with my bicycle leaning against a tree. Sue was lying, naked, on her front, sunbathing. Stefanie was sitting by the kitchen door, on a half-circle of old bricks, most of them hidden by the grass. She was playing with something; I shielded my eyes. It appeared to be a tortoise. No sign of Claire. I leaned out and announced myself.

The day unfolded slowly: I made myself some coffee and came out into the garden, in my shorts. Sue was in a sleepy mood, stretched out in the grass. We exchanged news in a perfunctory manner. She didn't seem to want to talk, and I said nothing about Chrissie. It wasn't quite the moment for intimate revelations—Claire had appeared above us, at the window next to mine, a large sketchbook in hand. She sat on the windowsill, her slim hands working quickly on the paper. I stood uneasily with my coffee, being, as I thought, sketched. Sue lay with her eyes shut, a large naked bulk. Stefanie poked at the tortoise with a blade of grass. 'Come on, tortoise,' she repeated. 'Come on. Come on.'

Sue's slightly distant manner had made me feel uncomfortable. I was here at David's, not at her behest. I started to feel like a spy; was that what they felt too? Perhaps it was all a big mistake. I didn't have to stay. A cycle tour of Britain took shape in my mind. Could I get somebody to send me a clean pair of trousers, *poste restante*, to Edinburgh? Well; it would be rather an exaggerated way to work off my pre-marital energies. Whenever I thought of

24

Chrissie, and proposing to her, I felt a surge of erotic excitement, as though it was a sexual, not a contractual offer.

The sun beat down on us. In the kitchen, the timer began to ping, at intervals. After a time, Sue lifted herself up and went indoors. She was a big, ungainly woman; that is, her movements were ungainly, rather like Chrissie's but on a larger scale. Some sort of city slovenliness overcame her when she stood to move. But in repose she was quite beautiful. Her large, attractive features, and her mass of dark hair, kept one's gaze off the sloppy posture. She was a thrilling listener, which wasn't always true of her husband. David told me his secrets, and I told Sue mine. It was a good arrangement.

With Sue indoors I came under Stefanie's suspicious gaze.

'Are you in the band?' she asked.

'No.' We looked at one another. She had Sue's big eyes, but someone else's paler colouring. She looked almost transparent. I said: 'I'm a friend of Mummy's.'

'Are you staying tonight?'

'I suppose so.' I looked up at Claire for help, but she was studying the finished sketch.

'Do you like tortoises?'

'Yes, very much,' I said.

'I don't know about this one. I think he hates me.'

'Oh surely not.'

She gave me a hard look.

'Lunch,' Sue called. I broke the pose, relieved, and went over to my bicycle to fetch a shirt from the saddlebag.

Over the meal I expanded to fill the silence. I still couldn't fathom the atmosphere; but I discovered that Claire was a Londoner now studying art at Norwich, that her parents were teachers, and that she'd heard of Stokesay House where I'd taught English to the immigrants. I began telling stories of those times, and some morbid inclination, possibly influenced by Stefanie's relentless stare, led me towards the old West Indian I'd visited that summer.

'We were doing a survey trying to find out how many of the local amenities the immigrant communities were using, parks and swimming pools and things. It was the children we were really supposed to find out about, but there weren't any at home in this particular house, only grandad. He insisted I come in. He sat down in the kitchen in a rocking chair; it should have been the porch of some Caribbean shanty home. But it was pitch dark. We were in the basement. No bulb. He wouldn't have anything to do with the questionnaire I'd brought. He wanted to tell my fortune, he took my hand and felt it, more than looked at it. You are a lucky person, he said—old voice out of the dark. He was stroking my hand. One door shuts, another opens, he was saying. And: had you opticals of marriage? I was puzzling over this—did he mean plans?—when he finally let go of my hand. I began to ask him questions from my clipboard, but he wouldn't answer. After a while I realized he was asleep. He was a little oddly slumped, though. Then the front door opened and a girl called out and came downstairs. She turned on a light in the hall. Came and shook him.'

I paused, savouring the ladies' attention, and rolled myself a cigarette.

'It's really very strange. He'd died as we were sitting there, while I was talking to him.'

There would have been a moment's silence then in honour of the dead, but for Stefanie.

'Why did he die?'

'Well . . . he was pretty old.'

'Was he very old?'

'Yes, he was an old man.'

I smiled at her serious gaze, which seemed less hostile. Sue caught my eye.

'How would you feel about a walk?'

'Can I come?' Stefanie asked at once. I saw Claire glance at Sue for guidance. 'You said we'd go to the beach,' said the child.

'No. Mummy's going for a walk with Jack, and we're going to try out your paints.'

'We'll go tomorrow, to the beach,' Sue said. 'We'll all go.'

'I want to hear about the man.'

'That's all I know,' I said.

'How did you know he was dead?'

Sue pushed back her chair. 'We can talk about it some other time.'

'I didn't know, at first,' I said, 'and the girl just had hysterics. I felt his pulse.' I stretched out my wrist across the table, palm up, to demonstrate.

'Jack, don't,' said Sue.

'Why not?'

'I'll tell you later.'

I drew back my hand and shrugged, smiling.

'Oh please,' said the child. 'Please! Show me! Please!' she pleaded, till I gave in, laughing.

As we drank our coffee the silence returned, and this time I couldn't find a way of breaking it. I didn't dare look at Sue for fear of catching her in some unguarded distress, the distress I thought I could sense in her mood. More than distress; anger. What had happened between her and David? Out of nowhere a voice resounded in my head, stammering: *women have no ma-ma-moral character. We do, that's why they hate us.* Of all unlikely people to come into my mind: they were Bromley's words, Bromley my part-time maths teacher; the school sage, and lifelong bachelor. At twelve I thought he was the happiest man I'd ever met and I had loved him as nobody since. I didn't think of him very often, but when I thought of my schooldays, when I thought of the past, I thought of Bomber Bromley.

I took a walk with Sue, along the Norfolk lanes. By contrast with the brooding peace of Bodmin Moor, its all-revealing light, Norfolk seemed benign and bland, dulling the senses with a soft white glare, an unreflecting void. The lunch lay heavy on my stomach. We strolled along the tarmac in the limpid sunshine, between high banks and hedgerows, and Sue took my hand as though she was about to tell me something.

'How's Chrissie?' she said.

'Fine. She's in Italy—didn't I tell you that?'

'Yes, you told me.'

She waited for more. For some reason my tongue was tied.

'I've missed you,' she said.

'Same here.' It came out rather lamely. 'What was all that, with Stef?' I asked. 'About the pulse.'

'Oh that.'

'It's not taboo, is it?'

'What do you mean—death? Good grief no, not at all, it's her favourite subject. She's always bringing me the tortoise, wanting to know if it's dead so we can have a little grave, and a cross with 'tortoise' on it. I might kill it myself to get some peace.' I grinned, with her. 'Show her how to take a pulse and she'll be trying it on everybody at the beach.' I studied her. 'Creeping up on sunbathers and grabbing them to see if they're dead.'

It sounded unlikely; I couldn't fathom this.

'What do you think of Claire?' It was Sue's turn to change the subject.

'How do you know her?'

'She was here last summer. Nice girl.'

'Very nice.'

'The local males fall in a pool of adoration at her feet.'

I made a non-committal noise. Sue wasn't looking at me. 'Is she really a nanny?'

'Not a trained one. But she looks after Steffie for me. I've got a lot of gigs this summer. Come to think of it, I met her through Diana. But she's a regular. In Cley, I mean.'

28

'*Cly?*' I echoed Sue's pronunciation. 'Is that how you say it?'

Sue nodded. '*Cly.* That's how the locals say it if you call it *Clay.*' She grinned. 'But if *you* say *Cly*, they'll call it *Clay* . . .'

'Fucked if you do, fucked if you don't,' I said, and felt sharply selfconscious saying it. My language often took on a strange turn when I was with Sue and David. Sue, as if in reproof, became more English; we kept passing in mid-Atlantic. But now she seemed to relax, and put an arm around me, amused. We stopped beside a gap in the banked foliage, where a gate gave onto an empty field.

'You did want me to come down?' I said.

'Very much.'

'I mean—being David's idea.'

'Why shouldn't I want you to come?'

'I know, but I rather gathered from his letter . . . that things had been a little strained.' She studied me, and said nothing. 'Is anything the matter?'

'Between me and David? No, love.'

There was a pause. 'He needs a job,' she said, and took her arm away. 'He talks about starting another book, then he doesn't do it, then he complains that I don't give him permission to fail.'

'He needs permission to fail?'

'Sure. Why not? The trouble is, he feels me standing over him, expecting results, when I don't—and I never say a word, not a word. So he tells me what my silence means and then he says how he feels about it, then he feels guilty and he tells me how I should really be chewing him out. And then he defends himself, as if I *had* chewed him out. And so forth. He talks all the time and then he calls my silence anger.' She shrugged it off, cheerful. 'Claire thinks he's mad.'

I thought some more. 'Does he fancy Claire?'

'What?'

'Well, you said . . . all the local males.'

'She's not his type.'

'Well, that's something,' I grinned. Sue wasn't smiling. She looked past me, down the lane.

'Whatever he gets up to with the ladies, he doesn't tell me about it, thank God.' I nodded. She eyed me, and turned back to the field. 'You wouldn't tell Chrissie, would you?'

'Nothing to tell.'

She was smiling once more; then she glanced at me. We'd had this conversation often enough before, but abruptly, under her gaze, I felt as if I was in the midst of a violent flirtation.

'You miss her?' She had my hand.

'I suppose.'

'Then you don't.' She looked amused.

Why had I answered so cagily? I tried to rescue myself. 'Well, I know she's coming back. I mean,' I paused, 'I'm very happy with her. I trust her.'

'Good. She's a smashing girl. Look after her.'

This should have been reassuring; it was the old Sue. But it wasn't reassuring. I pulled round, with my back to the metal gate. 'What if David gets the job?' I said. 'Will you go to Chicago?'

She continued to smile at me. 'Are you worried about *your* job?' she asked. 'I've no plans to sell the bookstore.' I shook my head, trying to show her I was serious. 'No, David doesn't really want to teach,' she said. 'Or write books. He wants another pig farm. I'm counting on you to talk him out of it.'

'Me? You know what he's like, he won't listen to me, he'll just spout Nietzsche. I mean, if I challenge him. Honestly.'

She was closing in again. 'You *should* challenge him. I do.'

'Of course. But it must be different for you because, I do think, when there's sex, there's . . . other ways of getting through to people. Surely.' I was babbling; then a phrase of David's rescued me. 'Which means that friendship . . .'

'Yes?'

I grinned. 'Quoting your husband: is the higher art.'

Sue nodded as though I'd said the right thing. She moved away from the gate, and led slowly up the lane. I followed. We were on a bend there, by the gate, and Sue was walking in the middle of the road, ahead of me. I realized she'd stopped. I couldn't see her face.

'Jack!'

As I caught up with her, I saw what had brought her up short. A van lay shattered on its roof, on the melting tarmac. The windscreen gaped open. Glass was all over the road, and a body lay between us and the van. The lane was quite still; no-one else was there, and the birds sang as if the body and the metal wreckage were all part of the pastoral scene, as if it all belonged. Instead it was grotesque and frightening, and unreal, as though prepared for view. At any moment a voice would cry 'Cut!' and the body would lift its head to look up at the unseen camera crew.

I ran forward to the spreadeagled figure. Blue, a dark blue boiler suit. The face bearded, and disfigured by the impact; face and hair were matted with blood.

'Is he dead?' Sue was still standing where she had caught her first glimpse of the crash.

'I don't know.' I looked round; hedgerows, sky. Something was missing. It was noise. For an instant it was as though the crash might yet come screeching at us round the corner of the small enclosed lane, to restore time. 'Is there anywhere to phone?'

'I'll find somewhere.' She ran back down the lane, the way we'd come.

I knelt over the body, feeling for his wrist. Contrary to what I'd told Steffie, I wasn't sure I could find a man's pulse. I couldn't feel anything, or hear a heartbeat when I put my head against his chest. He was still warm. I thought about the kiss of life, but his injuries were all too obviously to the head. He wasn't breathing.

What if there was someone else, trapped in the van? I hurried over to it. One of the doors was wide open. The van was empty. There were tools inside, and tubing, littering the seats and the upside-

down roof. Among them an open can of oil was oozing soundlessly.
I thought I could hear footsteps, in the lane. When I drew back to
look, relieved, there was no-one to be seen. But I had heard it: the
steady tread of someone walking towards me, footsteps on tarmac
coming from beyond the sharp, banked curve.

A man appeared, middle-aged, with his hair slicked down, walking
slowly, mechanically. I stood up.

'There's been an accident!' I called, and walked towards him.

His expression never changed. He was nattily dressed in suit and
tie, a loud suit, with a decorated waistcoat. As I neared him I saw
him waver and stop. Then—he was looking at me, not at the débris
behind me—he started out towards me with one hand incongruously
outstretched in greeting. I thought he must have misheard me, and
opened my mouth to repeat the message.

Until I saw his face, and stopped.

He was about to faint. I took his hand, the hand stretched out to
me. He held mine, studying me, and we stood there for a long
moment in the middle of the road, like longlost friends.

Then without warning his knees gave way and he fell to the
ground, almost taking me with him.

Kneeling, I shook him by the shoulder. The old boy's eyes were
open but there was no response. As I straightened up I realized my
right hand was still locked in his. I pulled away. His arm came up
without breaking the grip.

'Let go,' I heard myself say, in panic.

But he never blinked; he was out cold. I pulled at his fingers with
my other hand until I felt myself digging into his flesh. The bone
wouldn't give. I knelt beside him again, looking round for help. The
lane was quiet; no-one came, there was only the brilliant sunshine
and the tableau of the up-ended van. I could see skid marks now
where the machine had climbed the bank, and the gouged tree it had
hit before toppling over onto the road. I looked back at the man
gripping my hand and staring at the sky.

32

I couldn't work it out. Had he fainted when he saw the crash?

The eyes stared past me. Was it a fit? His face worked, briefly, alarmingly, and his mouth fell open, revealing bad teeth.

It was then that my own shock cleared. I stared at him, at his face, at his mouth, the brush moustache, the yellow teeth; amazed, in recognition. I knew who he was. It was Bromley. My old beloved Bromley.

IT TOOK ONE of the ambulance men both hands to prise the man's fingers from mine. What did he want from me, to cling so hard?

The little lane was full of people, cars, and noise, men shouting, doors slamming, onlookers helping to heave the shattered van to the side of the road. The ambulance orderlies must have thought I was holding Bromley's hand to comfort him, as they lifted him into the ambulance. 'He won't let go,' I said. They pulled us apart, rather roughly I thought, and slid Bromley into the depths of the waiting compartment. 'Can't I come with him?' 'No, sir, you can see,' one of them said, 'no room for passengers.' The shrouded body of the van driver was already in place beside staring Bromley. The ambulance men moved away. 'Where's he going?' I called, but they were climbing into their machine. A voice beside me said: 'The cottage hospital, I think you'll find.' I turned and saw a woman in a tweed suit, and beyond her, Sue, gazing at the ambulance, ignoring me. 'I'm Mrs Stevenson,' said the tweed suit, 'I work there. Would you like a lift?' Yes please, I said, eyeing Sue. 'I think I know him.' This time Sue turned, and stared at me.

The cottage hospital at Cley was an array of squat buildings, bungalows covered in creepers, and set back from the road. Bromley lay in a little, friendly, empty room with leaded windows darkened by the crowding vines. His head was propped up on a mass of pillows, and his pale eyes, still open, stared at the trees outside the window.

They had put him into hospital pyjamas.

We stood there watching him, as if at an audience: Mrs Stevenson by the bedhead, Sue behind me at the window. The police arrived, accompanied by the matron in medical uniform. The officer took up a position at the end of the bed; the matron softly shut the door. We all gazed at the peaceful features, awaiting an utterance. Bromley looked as though he was in thought, about to say something profound, but nothing came. He was still comatose.

'What was the name you said, sir?' The policeman glanced at me, then back at the face on the pillows.

'Bromley. John Bromley. He's a schoolmaster. He taught me.'

'Where was this?'

'The Arbor, it's called. It's in Somerset.'

'I see. You're positive about this, are you?'

'Yes.'

Like the others, I was still studying Bromley; it was so hard to believe he wasn't hearing all this, and it seemed almost impolite to look away. I realized the policeman had turned to me.

'Well, not entirely,' I said. 'Obviously. I haven't seen him for a good few years.' Only the brilliantined hair and the natty outfit had delayed my initial recognition. Bromley in the classroom was anything but natty. Clearly there was another side to him.

'I see. How is he, Mrs Stevenson?'

'No external injuries. That we could find.'

'He's got some documents with him. Letters,' the policeman was once more addressing the man in the bed, 'to a person called Sindacombe, at an address in Cromer. There's a Mrs Langley registered at this address: it's an hotel. And she confirms the description of, ah, Mr Sindacombe. He's been staying there with his wife.' He left a pause. 'She's known them quite some time, has Mrs Langley. Mrs Sindacombe, the wife, left the hotel yesterday. I have the home address from Mrs Langley. It's in Newmarket.' Another pause. 'I've made some preliminary enquiries, and it's in order. The

gentleman's a sales rep, works for Drummonds the seed merchants.'
The policeman screwed up his face, and cocked his head, politely
vexed. 'A Mr A F Sindacombe,' he said, without a glance in my
direction.

I stared hard at the indifferent face on the pillow. *Shut the door,
boy! Were you born in a cave?!* Bromley's favourite reproof—didn't
it fit the crooked lips, the face under the oddly slicked-down hair?

'We found this. In the van.' With a conjuror's flourish the
policeman produced something from behind his back, a bright straw
boater with a blue band, spotless, new. I tried to think back to the
van. Tubing, tools, the pool of oil. 'It doesn't fit the dead man's
head.' He moved swiftly to the bedside, opposite Mrs Stevenson.
'May I?' Without waiting for an answer he sat the straw hat on the
pomaded hair, jammed it down, and stood back.

From underneath the yellow brim, jaunty Bromley looked straight
past us at the sunlit afternoon beyond the window. Jaunty Sindacombe. The policeman stepped back to take up his position once
again, at the end of the bed.

'Do you think you could be mistaken?' he said.

The boater fitted perfectly. He was a sales representative, a seed
merchant on a seafront holiday. 'Yes,' I said. 'Yes, very possibly.'

'I spoke to Drummonds in Newmarket, they say he works part-
time for them. Used to farm his own place, till he went bust. Steady
sort of chap, they said.' The living statue in the bed confirmed it;
steady to the point of immobility. 'We haven't managed to make
contact with Mrs Sindacombe, as yet. But Mrs Langley is coming
here this afternoon to see Mr Sindacombe. And hopefully confirm
matters.'

There was a long pause. Sue spoke. 'You think he was in the
van?'

'If the hat belongs to him. He could have been thrown clear, you
see.'

And gone for help, found none, and wandered back in a daze,

perhaps.

'Yes. How odd,' I said. There was nothing to say; we stood there in a void. 'The thing is, I'd been thinking about Bromley, that's probably why I got confused.' No-one reacted. Not so much as a nod. They were gazing at Sindacombe.

I KNEW I must be wrong, it was easy enough to make that sort of mistake. I tried to summon up the faces of other schoolmasters I'd known. At first I thought I saw them clearly, but looking closer the portraits were smudged. Features stuck out, the whole was inexact. And anyway, what business was it of mine whether the man was Bromley or not? What was I to him? I hadn't even been one of his favourites, though I'd tried hard enough. He was a humorist. Everyone wanted his approval.

But I'd had the strange impression that the man in the lane knew me, before he fell, before I'd even recognized him. He'd offered me his hand, he'd studied me. Though as Sue pointed out later, the man was in a state of shock. He'd no idea who I was. This was a stranger; A F Sindacombe. Nevertheless I phoned the cottage hospital that afternoon, for confirmation. I'd spent twenty minutes on my knees, gripped by a stranger's hand as if for dear life—with Bromley's rotten teeth snarling up at me. I couldn't clear the memory.

When I came out into the back garden, the ladies were strewn about in the grass, in the last sunlight. Steffie was doodling at her paints, with Claire lying beside her. Sue was slumped in a deckchair. I stood for a moment on the grassy bricks, enjoying the air, the drama.

'Well apparently he's Sindacombe,' I said. 'According to the landlady.'

Sue shaded her eyes with one hand. 'He's still unconscious?'

'Yes. The doctor's been, says he's perfectly all right.'

'How can he be perfectly all right?' Sue's voice was faintly testy.

'I don't know. I mean he isn't hurt or anything.'

'Do they know if he was in the van?'

'Yes. Yes, he was in the van, they've traced the other man, the driver. They were together in a pub, in Wells. That's all I know. The other man's a plumber. Was a plumber. It was his van.'

'What was he doing with a plumber?'

Steffie giggled.

'Selling him something?' I said. 'I don't know.'

'It's not particularly funny, Steffie,' Sue said. The earlier, uncomfortable atmosphere was back. 'I knew this was coming,' said Sue, out of the silence. 'Something like this. I've been edgy all day.' None of us looked at her.

'I suppose,' I said, 'it can't be Bromley, can it. If the landlady's known him for ages.'

'How d'you know that?' Claire asked.

'That's what the policeman said. Didn't he?'

Sue nodded. 'For years.'

'You can write any old name in a hotel register,' said Claire. I was pleased. She seemed to be entering into the spirit of the thing.

'Well,' I said, 'there was a home address.'

'No Mrs Sindacombe yet?' Sue cut in.

I shook my head and continued, to Claire, 'And it's in order, whatever that means.'

'It means the Sindacombes exist,' said Sue firmly.

'Perhaps he's changed his name by deed poll,' Claire offered.

'Yes.' But I couldn't imagine why he would have. 'I'd know him if he spoke,' I said. 'He's got a bit of a stutter.' I tried my Bromley bark on Stefanie, abruptly: 'Shut the door, boy! Were you ba-ba-born in a cave?!'

A moment and then Steffie grinned. 'Do it again!'

I did, with relish.

'Do it again!'

'Did you get on with him?' Claire asked.

'No-one got on with him really,' I said, and for a while nobody followed it up, except Steffie.

'Do it again!' she yelped.

'What did he teach?'

'Nothing. He taught absolutely nothing, I mean he had no academic training. He was just a character.' Bromley: I tried to summon an image of him as I remembered him from The Arbor, as exact an image as I could, to confront this with the face on the hospital pillows. What I got was unexpectedly *dapper*, rather as one might picture one of the Three Men In A Boat fallen on hard times: a tall, slender person with a small head, small features, watery blue eyes in a long thin skull—a monocle would have suited him once—and the hair sparse but still wavy, sandy, reluctant to stay flat against the scalp. The little moustache; the teeth going, and the mouth with them. Yes, and he distracted you from the bad mouth by hugely raising and lowering the curly eyebrows whose sandy, grey-flecked colour matched his hair but which in their luxuriance seemed imported from another physiognomy, even stuck on; in fact they were the key to his personality, they were the bushy seat of surprise, of ambush, the salt-and-pepper source both of his rage and a promised tenderness; they made him endearingly gruff, remove them and he might be nothing, an irritable old man in need of false teeth. 'He used to be a cricketer before the war,' I said.

Sue was studying me. I couldn't keep the glee out of my voice when Bromley came to mind. 'I thought you hated your school,' said Sue.

'I did, yes. So did Bromley. He only liked animals.'

'Do it again!'

'Oh *Steffie!*'

I settled in the grass, a little distance from them, and let my head back to the ground, resting on cupped hands. Leaves, high above me, a beech tree in the church precinct over the wall. Beech leaves spotted with the dark coils of the caterpillars we used to keep in sweet jars; afternoons spent circling underneath the trees, scanning them leaf by leaf against the sky, when we should have been at the nets.

'I used to be something of a cricketer.'

Climbing up to Bromley's rooms, my arms laden with peculiar volumes, belonging to him. Washington, the spin bowler, had borrowed them first; he was the Bomber's favourite. And I was fast friends with Washington, we'd won the waltz contest together aged twelve, I the male, slimmer Washington the female. I used Washington to insinuate myself with Bromley; to get on the team. Bromley had rooms next to the upper dormitory, visited by favourites in dressing-gowns, to borrow or return the books. Washington borrowed one volume, I borrowed the rest in turn, addicted. Strange books. They didn't seem so at the time. Huge books almost two feet in length, with marbled leather at the corners, bound it felt as if in wood. They contained a tribute to the fallen dead of our school; on each page there was a photograph, a fine-looking young man sometimes in helmet or in officer's hat, sometimes bareheaded. There followed a description of a glorious career—a school career, that is, for these were young men fallen in the Great War, with little more than a commission and posthumous medals to add to their school record. There were scholarships and essay prizes, but mostly I marked the sports, the centuries against forgotten schools, the tally of goals scored during the final year. There must have been a date of death, a battlefield, I don't remember noticing. To me the books held nothing sombre, nothing tragic, only a glut of deeds, of goals, as good as *Wizard* or *The Eagle* could invent. I turned greedily from page to page, from face to face; I saw them as my contemporaries, twelve-year-olds; this was how my elders in the first eleven looked to me, they were adult, fully-formed, they too deserved heroic, fulsome tributes. Looking back it seems morbid. It wasn't, then. It was a feast.

Lugging those books, with aching arms, up the stairs to Bromley's upper chamber. We never discussed them. He held aloof. He had a vicious side to him which fascinated us and kept, I think, his colleagues at bay. Bromley ran the sports and only taught sporadically; but no-one interfered with this. He taught whatever took his fancy—maths, sometimes history, sometimes French, a language he declined to speak but wrote up on the blackboard. His main, his irreplaceable contribution was to school traditions. He invented them, or so it seemed to us. He certainly stage-managed them, the new boys' initiation ceremonies, the victory celebrations, the awarding of the school team colours, the 'Bust-Up' party on the final day of term. And the games: there was one called Convoys where we had to make our way through the woods above Taunton Vale to a large conifer dubbed 'Malta', while he and the school monitors played submarines, lurking in the undergrowth to sink you, 'sunk' if you were caught and touched. Bromley's submarine humour reached its peak in the annual school revue, which he wrote. In it we played the staff, in clothes we borrowed from them—'tradition' demanded it—while Bromley played the lord of misrule in the shape of Grub, a dirty schoolboy, his unruly hair tucked under a school cap. Bromley in shorts and squeaky voice, while we played out his mocking version of the year's events, in the adopted tones of his colleagues. It was a fool-feast, and only our gleeful over-acting kept its savagery in check. It was a golden time.

A vivid time. I can see prowling Bromley in the dormitory doorway as we turned from pummelling an odious boy called Green, Green whose hair we pulled because he wouldn't scream when we pulled it. As we fled to our respective beds, Green raised himself with weary middle-aged dignity, his mouth still ringed with traces of the chocolate cake he liked to eat after dark—the low smacking noises he made while he ate it were a gross provocation to us—and we watched him clamber slowly into bed. Bromley advanced in silence and, turning his back on Green, perched on the heavy metal rung at the foot of Green's bed. He waited, motionless.

'The Jews,' Bromley said at last, 'are known as the conscience of the world. Do you know why?' Silence. 'Because some of us fought and died to save young squits like you from a Jew-baiting ba-ba-bully-boy called Adolf Hitler. Who'd have been proud of you lot tonight.' I'd no idea what he meant. Perhaps some of the others knew Green was a Jew but I certainly didn't at the time. Bromley's words made precious little sense; but as far as we were concerned, he might as well have been speaking in Swahili. All we could think about was that despite his fearsome reputation he had never—it was said—actually used the cane. Now, judging from his tone, we might find out.

'Beating's too good for young brownshirts,' said Bromley, reading our thoughts. 'So the question is, what's to be done with you. Eh?' He paused. 'Well?'

Behind Bromley's back Green smiled a chocolate smile.

'Suppose . . .' Bromley went on, 'suppose I asked you all to write a letter home, beginning, *Dear Father* . . .'—he gazed round, taking his time—'. . . *Yesterday I bullied a Jew.* Would that be a suitable punishment, do you think?' Another pause. 'Mmh?'

The dormitory was silent; some of us perhaps reflecting that our fathers would be less troubled by this piece of news than by the unsolicited reminder that among their sons' school chums there would, in all likelihood, be Jews. For myself, I couldn't keep my eyes off Bromley. His small gaunt face, the brush moustache raised in distaste, reviewed the beds. I knew I mustn't meet his eyes but I wanted his attention, even now when danger threatened. Bromley met my stare, and held it. 'Well?'

'No, sir,' I said.

'*Not*, in your view,' he drawled, 'a suitable punishment?'

'No, sir.'

'Oh? Why not?'

'I haven't *got* a father.'

'No wonder,' said Bromley smoothly. 'Took one look at you, I dare say, and jumped out the window.'

The others shrieked with glee, grateful for a chance to change the mood and deflect Bromley's anger. It wasn't cruel laughter, it was just relief, but for the first time in my life I felt shame at my fatherlessness. Or rather no, that isn't quite true. I think I realized that until then I'd been proud of it, I'd felt special, a boy with a secret grief. Bromley, I'm sure—I was sure then too—knew little and cared less about my personal history, it was an automatic retort on his part, and I didn't love him any the less for his mockery. I loved him more: he might remember who I was, now.

And the dormitory mood had indeed been broken; no punishment ensued, perhaps because Bromley felt he'd already put the fear of God in us. He had, but now we detested Green as the conscience of the world, in Bromley's phrase, where before we'd only disliked him for failing to share his mother's monthly chocolate cake.

I was going to add that Bromley can't be blamed for that particular irony. On second thoughts I'm not so sure. He chose a boarding-schoolmaster's life for one reason only, it occurs to me: so that he could be a child again, as devious and immoral as we were. In Sue Harding's household it was, appropriately enough, little Steffie who best seemed to have grasped the Bromley mischief. When I entered her room that evening, specially summoned to say goodnight, she was gleaming with anticipation, bouncing up and down on the bed. 'Say it again!'

'Say what again?'

'About the cave.'

I put on the scowl and let fly at her; four times, before I was released.

'What does it mean?' she said.

'Well, caves don't have doors, do they, so if you were born in a cave you wouldn't know about shutting the door.'

She nodded, but this clearly didn't explain it to her. Or rather the logic added nothing to her pleasure. She was right, too. *Were you b-born in a cave?!* There was some obscure, delicious malice in it, which must have anchored the phrase in Bromley's mind and—for different reasons, perhaps—in mine. I could hear music from the sitting room as I came down the creaking stairs. Tin whistle, violin, melodeon, applause from a dozen pairs of hands: folkies recorded locally. I peeped in.

On the wall opposite, the street-scene painting glowed under lamplight. Sue was sitting beneath it on the sofa, head bowed attentively; Claire, dressed to kill, half leant half sat against the sofa arm, seemingly about to leave but loath to break Sue's concentration. At her feet were the saddlebags I'd brought in from my bike. 'Just going to put my trousers on,' I said, and fetched them.

'Not for our sakes.'

'No, I'm cold.' I slipped into the kitchen. 'Thanks all the same.'

I listened as I pulled off my shorts and put on my crumpled trousers. There was a silence. Steffie was humming, upstairs.

'You all right?' It was Claire; and then a pause.

'Drive carefully,' said Sue. I wondered what their glances were conveying, if anything. Claire called goodbye and went, without an answer, shutting the front door behind her.

'D'you know Tuscany?' I called.

'Tuscany? Yes.'

'Bromley fought a battle there once.' I returned to the sitting room, zipping up my trousers. 'Really; in the war. He used to draw it on the blackboard, like Hannibal versus the legions. Montepulciano was the place. I don't think it's recorded in the annals. There were only seven men involved. They all lived. I've actually been there, I went there from Pisa when I was on holiday, once, just out of curiosity.' I sat down on the sofa, conscious of Sue's gaze, begging me to change the subject. And yet I clung to it. I didn't think I'd imagined her flirtatiousness before we'd come across the shattered van; and I wasn't in a hurry to revive it. Take it easy,

David had said. 'He used to tell us all about his prisoner-of-war camp, he'd do a whole lesson as the camp Kommandant and we had to devise escape routes from the school, and make documents to get us across occupied France. It didn't do much for our French, but it was fun.' I grinned across her and began to rummage in my saddlebag. 'Look,' I said. 'I've brought you something.'

'What is it?'

I brought out a small bottle. 'Apricot Brandy.' Her favourite; filthy stuff. She smiled, pleased. 'Like some now?'

'Please.'

I found a glass and poured her some. None for myself, for the time being. She didn't say anything.

'Tell me about your gigs,' I said, 'the ones you mentioned.' She eyed me over the drink. 'No, I mean, what is it you're going to sing?' I said. Our eyes locked. 'What *are* you going to sing?'

On the record player, the instrumental was replaced by a quavery old man singing 'Foggy Dew' in authentic tones.

'Is it,' I nodded at the speakers, 'this sort of thing?'

'Uh huh. Some Norfolk songs.'

'Great,' I said.

'I've done them once or twice, in Norwich.'

'Give us one.'

'Later.'

'No, I'd like to hear one.'

But she sipped her brandy, unmoved.

'How do they go down?' I said.

'How d'you mean?'

'The songs.'

'How do they go down?' she mocked, sensing all too quickly what I meant.

'Yes. How do they go down.' It was too late to back off. 'I mean, since you're not a local.'

The quavery voice from the record player lurched into another verse.

'Since I'm not a local what?' said Sue casually into her glass.

'Well, don't they think it's poaching?'

'Everybody poaches folk songs.' There was a silence. 'You mean, because I'm an American I'm not supposed to sing them?'

I felt myself drawn into the turbulence, even willing it, as a last obstacle to whatever lay beyond it. 'No,' I said. 'No. It's nothing to do with your being American.'

''Cause I'm not . . . what, then?'

'Well, you know how it is: in Aguas Calientes they don' like strangers . . .' I battled on, adding in a deeper south-of-the-border voice, 'in Aguas Calientes they don' like *nobody*.'

'Listen, no-one round here treats me like a freak. Nobody cares. It's just a lot of people who like folk songs and everyone gets up and sings a song, any old song.' I nodded. 'I don't pretend to be British, I don't pretend to be anything!' Her voice was getting louder. 'Remember when I first came over, how I tried to get rid of the accent so I could play British roles? And how you sneered? Remember?' Had I sneered? I remembered how much I'd loved her soft Virginian tones, now studiously avoided along with the Southern expressions she used to parade for us. Of a prominent member of the company she'd say he was 'as nervous as a long-tailed cat in a room full of rocking chairs,' and once, to everyone's guilty delight, 'why, he's sweatin' like a nigger writin' cheques!' Now the languid drawl had gone, the vowels were sulphurous and short. What she didn't need, she was telling me roundly, was people giving her all this shit about where you fit in: 'Nobody cares that much. They've got nice songs here, they like for people to sing them and that's all they ask. It's helping keep the songs alive. Or don't you understand that?' I did. She was right.

We paused. 'D'you want to know what I really think?' I said.

'No,' she said, and went into the kitchen to wash out her glass.

I felt old habits closing in on me, and the same bumptious manner that overcame me when I argued with Chrissie, finding myself proposing theories I didn't even believe in, just to provoke. The next round was a lot slower, and nastier. It wasn't helped by the fact that Sue stayed in the kitchen, nibbling at some grapes, while I stayed on the sofa. We could see each other through the open doorway. From music we moved on to the subject of country living, where I felt on firmer ground. I had no time for the whole homespun hayseed homesteading propaganda that Sue now liked to expound. It was all new to her, a new craze, far removed from David's sombre quest for silence with his pigs. To Sue it was hope, a community, she wanted one pig and lots of people; David wanted one person and lots of pigs. Either way it seemed to me absurd, a living diorama from some arts and crafts museum. We slugged ourselves to a standstill.

'I'm only objecting to the word,' I said.

'What word.'

'Culture. I'm only objecting to the word.' I struck a match and held my tiny cigarette end over the flame. Burning ash fell on the sofa. 'The last time this place had a culture was the Middle Ages.'

'Fuck the Middle Ages.'

'Right,' I said, stubbed out the cigarette butt and began to roll another.

'Come in here. Jack.'

'Why don't you come in here? This is the living room.'

'It's my house.' She gazed at me. 'Please.' I gazed back. 'Come here and tell me about the Middle Ages.'

Abandoning my tobacco tin, I stood and walked to the kitchen door. Sue was plaiting the grape stems.

'In the Middle Ages,' I began.

'Yes?' She went on plaiting. Then she looked up, and eyed me for a moment. 'Oh go away.' There was a silence.

'Half a dozen people in a folk club,' I mocked, 'singing sea shanties, that's not a bloody culture. Growing vegetables and keeping goats on little bits of string.'

She laughed. 'What is it, then?'

46

'Come on. You know what I'm talking about.' Sue ignored me. I patted my pockets for the missing tobacco, and went back to the sofa to fetch it. 'You really are a bitch,' I murmured under my breath and, louder: 'If you came here in the Middle Ages—'

She made a fed-up whiny noise, sounding like Steffie.

'—and you'd gone up to the architect of any of these churches,' I came back to the doorway, unravelling tobacco, 'and you'd said, wouldn't you like to build us a church in London? They'd have said: up yours.'

'Up yours?'

'That's right.' I picked angrily at the dry, flaking strands. 'Have you got any cigarettes?'

There was a pause. 'D'you want to smoke some grass?' she said. Caution, now. 'Norfolk Green,' she grinned.

Caution. 'Not for me, thanks.' I pursued my argument. 'They had money. Simple as that: money. That's what I mean. They said up yours.'

'In Latin.'

'No, in Anglo bloody Saxon.' I gazed balefully at her; she had no right to be offering me . . . well, what I thought she was really offering me. 'Your lot,' I said, and waited for her attention.

'My lot?'

'Your lot would be on the London train before you could say telly series.'

It was her turn to look baleful. 'So . . . *what?*'

'That's all I'm trying to say.'

'No shit,' she queried with studied vagueness, and walked out of the kitchen. It wasn't till next day that I found out she hadn't been offering me what I thought, at all.

WE WALKED OUT onto Blakeney Point, over the dunes, and settled on a narrow shoal, among the tourists; there was little choice.

We lay facing the shore, the busy port, the caravans. The windmill on the beach at Cley shone in the distance. Grasses drooped from the tussocks behind us. Steffie paddled; Sue snuggled into the sand. I had my Sufi book with me, and I stared dully at the same page, in the sun.

It wasn't really country living I disliked at the time. It was the attitudes, the whole charade that went with it. One of my closest friends from school dropped out of art college and became a fisherman near Felixstowe. I went out with him once or twice and helped to haul in the gigantic, squirming cod, and took the helm on the way home while Jamie and his mates ripped the heads and innards from the fish, flinging them to the gulls as they swooped to catch the flesh before it hit the water. Jamie wore a beard, a regulation blue pullover, fingered a melodeon; he was playing the local lad; keeping bees, and boozing, Chinese takeaway meals on the dock, discussing last night's TV. He was playing it well enough. But I resented being left to mime the urban spaceman with his manic smile. I certainly didn't believe you could invent or re-invent a way of life in its own name alone; it was a by-product of power or it was nothing, sheer nostalgia, so I would declare. Folk culture made me sick. But this was something other than a settled prejudice. As David put it, my steamy angulations were a little stroppy. I was easily wrought up.

And easily becalmed again. I'd made it up with Sue, the morning after, over breakfast, by grabbing her guitar and busking an earnest Norfolk ditty. I also said sorry. 'Oh *my*,' she said, indulging me, 'you really get aggressive.' 'Host'le,' I asked, 'do I get host'le?' She laughed and let it go. 'I've spoken to the matron, at the hospital,' she said, and I was touched that she'd taken the trouble, after all my gabbing about Bromley. 'And?' 'Nothing.'

'Ring the school,' Sue suggested as we lay on the sandbank. 'Find out for certain.'

'Yes.'

'Why don't you, then?'

'There won't be anyone there, it's the holidays.' The school buildings nestling in the rhododendrons; the pavilion and the grounds, the beeches. 'I suppose there might be somebody. It would be awful, wouldn't it, if it was Bromley lying here, in a coma, and nobody knew.' The truth was, I hadn't been thinking about the man in the cottage hospital. It wasn't Bromley.

Sue was lying with her eyes shut. 'Where's Claire gone?'

'I don't know.' Somewhere down the beach the tourists' children laughed and shrieked, jumping off sand dunes. 'She's getting something to drink.'

'Where's Steffie?'

'She's there, she's right there.' My gaze lingered on the waterline, where Steffie was watching the boats. I sensed that Sue was looking at me.

'D'you like the sun?' she said.

'Yes. Very much.'

'Do you?'

'Don't *you*?'

'Why are you wearing those shoes, that's what *I* want to know,' she said.

'They're comfortable.' They were my antique cycling shoes, loafers, battered.

'You like wearing dirty shoes.'

'Not particularly.'

She smiled. 'What shall we do?'

'Have a swim.'

Sue was looking fondly at me, brother-and-sisterly; this was all right. 'Sing something,' she said. 'Sing me a song.'

'Me?'

She purred, stretching happily. 'I'm glad you've come.' There was a pause. 'Claire fancies you like mad.'

I studied her, suspicious but aroused. It was such a big face. It was just a very big face, it was a married face, even when she was being whimsical.

'Oh?'

'She told me.'

'You're making it up,' I said. She nodded, to tease me, and I turned away, smiling, annoyed.

'Jack, I'm not. I promise, swear to die. She thinks you're very sexy.'

The teasing crassness of it. 'I thought you were telling me to look after Chrissie.'

'And so you will, I'm sure.' But her smile said: I can see through you. My fingers dug under the sand; my hands felt numb, sand-numb. This wasn't right, and yet it was the pay-off to so many conversations Sue and I had had. Among her divorcee friends drifting in and out of the London apartment, I was the eligible boy whose hands, amusingly, were tied, who'd been attached since he was eighteen but was still so absurdly young—and could be teased and dallied with. Sue leaned over and took my book. I pulled my hands out of the sand and snatched it back. She eyed me, grinning. The whole thing was unreal; neither of us was promiscuous.

'Mind you,' I said, 'I've no idea what Chrissie gets up to, every summer.'

But I was thinking of a letter written to me by another school-friend, after he'd got married at twenty-one: the most surprising thing about marriage, he wrote, is the sense of freedom. I looked over at Sue. She was still smiling at my possessiveness about the book.

'It's mine,' I said.

'What is it?'

'It's a book on Sufism.' Squinting against the sun, I held it up briefly as though to assure her that the cover was the best of it.

'Sufism?'

'Sufi-ism. The Sufis.'

She laughed, at the sounds. 'It's a religion,' I said, 'without a name: even Sufism isn't its real name.'

'I see.'

'Do you?' I said, but Sue only went on smiling. 'It's a first-rate religion, they have no names—no titles, that is—no services, no rules, no bible, and no God.' It sounded impressive, though I wasn't too sure of my facts.

'So what is it?' She smiled; the topic hovered in the dull heat, ready to evaporate. 'What do you do, then? If you're a Sufi?'

'Anything. It's simply handed down, in sayings. And stories.' I paused. 'D'you want to hear one?'

'Is it long?'

'No, they're all short.'

'Go on, then.'

I hesitated, and felt foolish under her gaze.

'Oh come on,' she said. 'Either you are a Sufi or you aren't.'

'No,' I said, 'I didn't say I was a Sufi.'

'Didn't you?' She waited for me. 'Well, I don't care.' And she flopped back onto the sand. I watched her for a while.

'Has she got a feller?' I said. Sue nodded faintly, with barely a smile. 'Here?'

Sue shook her head. 'In London.' Abruptly, she changed tone. 'What's the child doing?'

I glanced. 'Swimming.'

'Is she all right?' Sue sat up, so as to see her. 'Steffie!'

'She's only paddling.'

Sue eased back again, nearer to me, and took my hand. I sensed danger.

'There's one very short Sufi saying,' I said quickly.

'Yes?'

'Which goes . . . *It is not in fact so.*'

Sue surprised me by breaking into peals of delighted laughter. I'd thought it was obscurely apt, but not that apt. In the process she relinquished my hand.

'I like it!' she said. 'I like it.' When she calmed down, she was gazing at me again. 'You're a very funny man,' she said, nicely.

The sound of splashing became more distinct. Stefanie seemed to be dogpaddling rather wildly, beating at the water. She was some ten or fifteen yards into the sound, with a low sandbank beyond her, parallel to the shore. It looked safe enough.

'Are you all right?' I called.

Sue got to her feet, alarmed, before the child could answer. 'Steffie? Are you all right?'

'No,' came an unhappy voice, from the water.

'She's perfectly all right,' said Sue drily as I rose to my feet. We watched her for a moment. I wasn't convinced, and I set off down the beach at a run, losing my shoes on the way. 'Jack!' Sue called, to stop me, but I was launched. I plunged in and made for the jerking figure ahead of me. The girl was sobbing now. 'Mummy!' she yelled. I could hear footsteps on the beach behind me.

I reached Stefanie and ignored a flailing blow across the head; we both swallowed water as I struggled to lock an arm around her. Lifesaving class had been compulsory at The Arbor. All I could remember was pulling the mock-victim backwards.

'Don't struggle—Steffie!—limp, go limp!' I shouted. I was starting to go limp myself. And then I got her. As I kicked out to send us back towards the shore, my feet hit ground, hard. I stood up, bewildered, pulling the child up with me. 'You can stand,' I said. The water came up to my ribs; to her upper arms. I stared at her.

'I can't!' she wailed.

'You can! You're standing!'

'Mummy!'

I looked at her, confused. 'Have you got cramp? Steffie?'

She stared back, shivering. Suddenly she burst into tears again and her head sank into the water, arms working to stay clear of the waves.

'Put your feet down,' I said.

'I've got cramp.'

I lost my temper. 'Put your feet down!'

After a moment, she did, and stood up without difficulty, out of the water, sobbing silently. I felt ashamed of my outburst, and looked up at the beach. We had an audience. And Claire was running along the sand towards us, carrying Pepsi.

'I've got cramp,' wept Steffie, softly.

'I'M GOING TO Diana's this afternoon. You can come if you want.'

Sue was addressing Stefanie, on the front passenger seat beside her. It was intolerably hot in the car, a dusty, ill-kempt Triumph Vitesse. Claire and I sat in the back, flushed and tense.

'I'll take Steffie,' Claire offered.

'That's all right, Claire.'

'I want to stay,' said Steffie.

'Where?' Sue asked fiercely. '*Where* d'you want to stay?' A glance from her mother and Steffie backed down. 'Do that again and it's the last time you go to the beach. Do you hear? I told you to stay by the shore.'

'Actually, I don't think she was in any danger,' I said. I thought of adding, for Sue's benefit, that it was 'not in fact so', but I thought better of it. Steffie started to cry again, in self-pity.

'That's not the point.' Sue took her eyes off the road, and Claire and I instinctively reached for something to hold onto. 'She made it look like she was drowning. Next time you can howl till you're blue in the face,' she told the child. 'If it's not drowning it's appendicitis. And where's your watch?'

'At home.'

Sue grunted. 'Lose your head next.'

A car loomed up in front of us. 'Well, I don't know,' I began, trying to cool things down.

'You knew you could stand!' Sue resumed.

'I didn't!'

'She simply panicked,' I said.

'Panicked my ass. I know why she did it and so do you.'

Only one thing came to mind: Steffie put out by Mummy's tête-à-tête, by an imagined dalliance, was that what Sue meant? But as I recalled it, Steffie's crisis had only begun when Sue had shouted a quite unnecessary are-you-all-right? to her, and then ignored the child's prompt wail of distress.

'Mrs Harding,' Claire began.

'Don't give me panicked,' Sue added to me for good measure. There was a pause. She glanced round at Claire, and back to the road. 'It wasn't your fault. I should have been watching Steffie. And for God's sakes don't address me that way.' The driver in front slowed; Sue snarled at him. 'Well, are you going to turn or aren't you?'

We braked. I had to escape. 'Could we . . . do you think I could jump out near the cottage hospital?'

'Up to you.'

'Can I come?' Steffie piped up.

'No you can't,' said Sue. The car in front finally eased onto the side of the road. Sue leaned out of the window. 'Signals!' We drove on in silence. 'Yes all right,' she said, suddenly.

The hospital was dark and cool, and empty. Steffie hovered as I waited for the matron. I didn't quite know what to say to the girl when I was alone with her; I could ask whether she missed America, but either way the answer would be inauspicious for one or other of her parents. I was flattered that she'd wanted to come with me; I was probably the lesser of two evils that day. Or perhaps she felt a morbid curiosity about the body in the bed. Luckily it was Mrs Stevenson, less fearsome than the matron, who appeared first. There was no change in the patient, apparently, only an intermittent fluttering of the eyelids.

'Blepharoclonus, the doctor said.'

'Ah.'

We fled into the little room and shut the door behind us. A hydrangea plant had been introduced, breaking the bareness of the room, on a table by the window; its deep reflective blue uneasy in the sunlight. We crept round to the end of the bed.

The figure sat erect, as ever, eyes fixed on the window and the blue petals framed in it. But Bromley's expression had changed. Sindacombe's, I should say; but with this look on his face I couldn't think of anyone but Bromley. He looked stern. He rebuked the midday sun, he was trying to hold onto something, something more important than the playful light invited. This was grim-visaged Bromley, Bomber Bromley, nicknamed—so we were told—after a wartime plane, the Bromley bomber. Now it seemed apt. He looked as if he was about to rain destruction, to put on the black cap and deliver sentence.

But he was silent, as before. Had he eaten? How did they feed him? It was nearly twenty-four hours. I pulled out the chair beside the bedhead and sat near him, studying the face.

Was it a face I knew, the face I'd known? Or only a similar face—belonging, perhaps, to a similar breed of man, caustic, fantastical? Or to a very different kind of man, steady old Sindacombe? What could be read from features? Features so inert, frame-frozen: all the easier to read, or all the harder? As a teenager I'd studied snapshots of my father, peered intently at the blur of face—the results of my mother's Box Brownie work were never very sharp—and tried to picture it, my father's face, in different situations. Angry, absorbed, excited. Making love. Mother had given me an old school photograph he'd kept, and this was the one I studied hardest, trying to make the smooth-skinned, raw-boned eaglet's face, all jutting features, fit the only story I had of my father's early years: caught *in flagrante* fornicating with some local tart—as Mother described it—schoolboy Richard faced expulsion and disgrace. 'I've only got one thing to ask you, Thurgo,' the headmaster had said. 'Was it love or lust, boy?' Which answer would save him? 'Love, sir,' my father had answered, and guessed right. 'Dishonesty was rewarded,' Mother commented drily when she told this cautionary tale, 'and your father was reprieved.'

But *was* it dishonesty? The Richard-face in the school photo insisted 'love, sir' when I questioned it, all I could see in it was love (blind and extravagant, as I construed it from the face) despite its coarse planes, its rapaciousness, its ugliness in fact, its splendid boldness, nose like a promontory, chin huge, eyes brutishly small and close-set, a far cry from my obstinately, maddeningly girlish looks, wide-eyed, snub-nosed and smudge-lipped beneath the heavy gilt-and-bronze hair that I was genuinely grateful for—and most proud of when it was drying, as it was now after my impromptu dip, into straight, slickly glinting locks of copper wire. Father's head grew a wild aboriginal thatch like a clump of fire-blackened gorse. And if I felt no kinship with the look of him, it was equally true that I felt no loss of kinship, gazing at his face; to all intents and purposes I'd never known the man, I hadn't one surviving memory of him. It could as easily have been a snapshot of a great-grandfather, and perhaps this was why I had no desire, no need for him to look like me, though I would have preferred to look like him, piratical, already craggy at eighteen—and soon to join the RAF, soon to be bundled willy-nilly into high adventure and, in due course, into the next snapshot in my collection, showing him with Molly, bride and groom in uniform . . . huge groom and little tubby Molly-bride . . .

Stefanie's fidgeting brought me back to the present. She was by the window, looking at the floor, uncomfortable. I thought of the painting in Sue's sitting room, of the child silhouetted in the high doorway. 'Want to go home?' She nodded, though not very firmly. 'All right,' I said.

I was still mesmerized by the hard face beside me; I couldn't resist one brief try to rouse him. I leant forward. 'John?' There was no

56

response. 'John Bromley...'

Stefanie was whispering behind me. 'What are you doing?'

Bromley stared ahead, and I sat fixedly on the bed before him, in the coolness, the soporific stillness, without moving, as though the coma were contagious. At some point the door opened. Claire's head, her blonde hair swinging, appeared. She looked at the patient and smiled questioningly at me. I sat dumbly.

Claire nodded at Stefanie. 'Sue thought she might have had enough.' I smiled agreement, a little ashamed at having allowed her to come. But Stefanie wandered off to the window again as if in no hurry to return home.

'Out of there, please!' came a voice from the corridor. 'Everyone out!' The footsteps swept on past.

'Come on, Stef.'

'You go ahead,' I said. 'I only want a minute.' They left me with scowling, disapproving Bromley.

The instant the door shut I could feel the mood change, and I fought it: I was Jack Thurgo, a grown-up, *not* a child called to answer for a transgression, alone in the room now with the master in charge. It was a losing battle, try as I might to laugh at the situation; in fact it was all I could do not to glance round in search of the small cane Bromley kept on his bookshelves. Years after we left The Arbor a friend named Trevelyan had told me that this cane, supposedly just for show, had indeed been put to use—and on Trevelyan, with the words 'I won't say this is going to hurt me more than it hurts you, because it isn't, it's only going to hurt *you*.'

Trevelyan it was who got me into Bromley's disfavour. He was a trouble-maker, 'bolshy' was the usual term, though a less likely bolshevik never wore school uniform. I myself was not a trouble-maker; except by association. This was my mistake. Trev rose through chastisement to a glittering school career. I never made school monitor, I was the wrong material, unfit for punishment or reward. When we went on together to public school, I watched

Trevelyan pupate like one of our Somerset caterpillars, emerging from dirty, rebellious fag (Bromley's 'Grub') to spread his wings as school prefect and head of the house. During his reign the house caught fire, but since the great Trevelyan was himself responsible—he'd set light to his room while cooking breakfast—no-one seemed to mind too much. Shortly afterwards, while the building was still swathed in scaffolding, some boy appeared at night outside the assistant matron's bedroom window and, seeing her undressing in the darkened room, climbed in and made an unsuccessful grab for her before escaping down the planking, unidentified. Trevelyan, head of house, was appointed to investigate the matter; the housemaster ordered him to find the culprit at all costs; the culprit was of course Trevelyan. What was he to do? Dr Bryans had told him the honour of the school was at stake. So he duly interrogated every boy of appropriate size and ambition, and reported a blank. This wouldn't do: the housemaster insisted on results. Trevelyan was empowered to impose whatever sanctions he thought fit. Trevelyan did, unperturbed. Privileges were taken away, stage by stage, from every boy, until at last we spent the summer afternoons confined and moaning, singly, in our rooms, without shaming the would-be rapist into a confession—all summer long Trevelyan revelled in his freedom while we sweltered indoors. But as sadists go he was only an amateur, as he discovered on the last day of term, during his farewell interview with Dr Bryans. The housemaster congratulated him on an outstanding spell as head of the house, adding, 'D'you know when I first knew you'd make the grade, Trevelyan?' 'Sir?' 'The day you didn't own up to assaulting the assistant matron!'

With Trev as a teacher I could have gone far at school. Instead I was his tool, from the beginning. One day Bromley had decreed a fielding practice, which I dreaded, it was my weak point. Trevelyan too was all for ducking it; he was the wicketkeeper, and he wanted to be bowled at in the nets. I agreed. Bromley came upon us. Trev's excuse stood up, as usual—he was getting fielding practice;

mine didn't, and I was relegated to the second team, for the rest of the term. But I had my revenge on Bromley. It was slow in coming, and I was patient. The Bomber's teaching was of course his weak point, though he tyrannized and tickled us into forgetting that. Finally he slipped up; he'd chosen maths that day, my home ground, and it was a question he'd chalked up on the board the previous evening, to save himself bother in the morning, that gave me my chance. *Diophantes*, it ran, *passed one sixth of his life in childhood, one twelfth in youth, one seventh more as a bachelor. Five years after his marriage, a son was born who died five years before his father, at half the age his father finally reached. How old was Diophantes when he died?* This was child's play. I quickly ran through the equations, and then found the numbers rather odd. Diophantes apparently died at the age of ninety-three years, three months, twenty-nine days, fourteen hours, eleven minutes and sixteen point six recurring seconds. It began to dawn on me that pleasing—and plausible—as this was (if you ignored the recurring .6 of a second, recurring and deferring death over and over like Zeno's ever-travelling arrow, hypnotized by numbers), it was quite unlike the comfortable kind of answer called for by our textbooks. I looked back at my workings. The search for Diophantes' 'moment "x"' resolved itself initially as $x - 5 - (\frac{33x}{84} + 5) = \frac{x}{2}$. This boiled down to $x = \frac{10}{9} \times 84$. Staring at it, I saw that if x equalled *nine* over nine times eighty-four, instead of ten over nine, this gave the sort of round number to be expected. My classmates were still labouring over their graph paper; I looked back at the blackboard. *Five years after his marriage, a son was born who died five years before his father*—but what if Bromley had repeated 'five' in error? If the second figure was four, not five, it would give nine over nine in the last equation, and Diophantes would have died at an age more suitable to schoolboy sums. At eighty-four exactly. 'Sir!'

And Bromley, as it happened, didn't have the book with him, the book from which he'd copied out the question. He only had the answer: eighty-four. And I wasn't going to help him. To my joy, he had to struggle through the equations himself, fuming, to trace his error, while everybody sniggered and I sat in triumph. Bromley did his best to turn the tables, of course. 'The question *isn't*,' he roared, 'whether *I've* got it right or wrong. The question is . . .' and here he wrote the key words hugely on the blackboard, 'whether the wretched halfwit Diophantes, this algebraic worm who spent a mere $\frac{12}{x}$, one *seventh* of his earthly existence, as a bachelor: whether *he* got it right or wrong!' We knew Bromley's views on marriage. 'Wrong!' we roared back at him. Bromley wrote it up furiously, breaking chalk as he went, $\frac{1}{7}$*bachelor=wrong*, $\frac{7}{7}$*bachelor=right*, and let us out ten minutes early.

A knock at the door. I stood at once and pushed back the chair. The knock came again. 'Come in,' I said.

The door opened slowly and a woman came in, or rather slid in. She pressed herself against the wall as if to steady herself and, it seemed, to put more distance between herself and the bed than the little room afforded. We stared at each other but she didn't seem to be taking me in. She was middle-aged, and dressed in mauve. The door remained open.

'Mrs—' I said, and groped for the name; Sindacombe.

'Langley,' she supplied, before I could get the word out. *Lengley*. There was an accent, but I couldn't place it for a while. She glanced at the bed, fearfully, then at me, seeming to focus. 'How is he?' she said. I could only shrug. She looked back at the bed. 'You know Arthur?' *Arsur*, she pronounced it.

I followed her gaze: Arthur. A F Sindacombe. I hesitated. 'You, ah,' I said. 'He was staying with you?' But she had broken the spell that held her to the back wall, and was advancing on the bed.

'You know what it is, an oculogyric crisis?' She sounded German. 'O-cu-lo-gyric,' she repeated, and brought a slip of paper from her bag on which the word was written. We looked at it together.

'A what?' I said. 'I don't, no. What is it?'

'Neither do I.' She leant over him. 'Arssur...' she whispered, rather as I had earlier, but he didn't answer to this name either. The woman was gazing at him with—surely—more than a landlady's concern for a stricken guest. And murmuring his name. Ah sir, she seemed to be repeating.

'I don't think he can hear you.'

This misled her. 'Arthur!' she cried, raising her voice an octave. There was no reaction from the bed, but the hospital seemed to come alive around us. Footsteps hurried down the corridor, I heard the matron's voice, 'Don't *shout* at him, you silly woman!' There was no escape. She surged into the room with Mrs Stevenson in tow, and took me in, amazed.

'What's he doing here?' she demanded. 'I asked you to go away. You haven't been here all this time, have you?'

'I came back,' I said.

'You're lying!' she announced. It was odd; I had a growing feeling that I wasn't the only one. 'Who *are* you?'

'Please . . .' I said. Mrs Langley looked on, dazed. The matron turned to her.

'Who *is* he?' she insisted.

'Look, I'll go.'

Outside the cottage hospital I lurked beneath the trees, waiting for the mauve dress, alias Mrs Langley. It was a long wait and I'd missed lunch, but I was sustained by the sense of detective work. Eventually she emerged, then seemed to lose her way among the buildings. When she found the path again I ran across the grass and caught up with her in the drive. She was in tears.

THE ENCOUNTER LEFT me slightly abashed. Mrs Langley was too overwrought for close enquiry, and all I got was a confusing, plausible rigmarole about the Sindacombes, how Mrs Sindacombe had brought her mother to the seaside, how Arthur hadn't liked the seaside, how Mother had died and Arthur had decided he *did* like the seaside. Poor, poor Arthur. There was only one problem. The man in the bed was Bromley. I hurried back to the cottage, where the women were washing up, and comandeered the phone; got the number from directory enquiries and dialled the school. Steffie sat opposite me, infected by my curiosity. A girl answered, full of life, incongruous—I couldn't remember anyone at The Arbor under forty. And she brimmed with information. I called for a pen and pad, and Steffie helped me out while I listened. The cheery, chatty young voice consigned my precious memories, my image of the school, to the inaccessible past, but there was no time to attend to this: the news she gave was startling, in one respect. My voice must have communicated this, because Sue came to the kitchen doorway and stood watching as I signed off.

'Well?'

'Bromley's retired,' I said slowly. 'He lives in Wales.'

'In Wells?' said Sue sharply. 'That's down the road.'

'In Wales. Radnorshire somewhere, I've got the address.'

Sue stared as my grin swelled, as I took it in.

'He's married,' I explained. 'He's gone and got married!' I whooped for all my schoolfriends. That wretched halfwit Diophantes—the algebraic worm—had been right after all. A little premature, perhaps, at $\frac{x}{6} + \frac{x}{12} + \frac{x}{7}$ years, or 33 precisely, married a good deal earlier than Bromley. But right!

'Are they on the phone?' Sue asked.

I nodded, as the full force of it hit me. 'Oh Lord,' I said.

'What's wrong?'

'Well: it's a dirty weekend! It's obvious. He's having a dirty weekend, that's what he's up to.'

'But Mrs Langley knows him, Jack. Knows Sindacombe.'

'Of course she does,' I said. 'She's the lady in question.'

Sue stared at me.

'Bromley,' I said, 'and Mrs Langley. Don't you understand? There *is* no Mr *or* Mrs Sindacombe.'

'Well, what about the Sindacombe address? He wouldn't *need* a real address. Just think about it, Jack. The police confirmed it.'

I thought about it. She was right. And yet: 'Arthur F Sindacombe'—it was pure Bromley. No prizes for guessing what the 'F' stood for.

'And if his wife's hundreds of miles away in Wales, he wouldn't really need a false identity.'

'You don't know Bromley,' I said.

'I don't see why he'd take a real person's name. Do you?'

'Could be all sorts of reasons. Remember, we only have Mrs Langley's word that he's Sindacombe.'

'And letters, Jack. The police found letters on him.'

'That's part of his cover.' It sounded thin, even to me. But the face on the pillow wouldn't let me go.

'All right then,' Sue said after a moment, slowly. 'Ring him.'

'At home?' She didn't seem to have grasped the situation. 'And get his wife? Sue, that's up to the police.'

'It's up to you. They think he's Sindacombe. Good grief, if you believe he's lying here in hospital and his wife doesn't know...'

'He isn't dying. He's bound to come round. Isn't he?'

No-one said anything.

'Look, what's an oculogyric crisis?'

Luckily there was a hypochondriac in the house, or rather his books. David was a meticulous sufferer, and his dictionaries bore witness to it. Oculogyria, we discovered, was some sort of staring fit, of *'uncontrollable rigidity'*. 'See Amimia...' Amimia turned out to be *'the loss of mimetic, histrionic, and expressive capacities. See also Gegenhalten; Paratonia; Coma; Oculogyria.'* We were going round in circles. It didn't say how permanent any of them were. 'The point is this,' I said. 'If he comes round he'll go home, no-one will be any the wiser. If I ring up and put my foot in it, bang goes the double life.' Despite herself Sue was beginning to grin. 'He'll have had it...' I said, 'marriage up the spout...' I was laughing too; this was absurd ... *Sir? How much of his $\frac{x}{84}$ should Diophantes have spent on adultery, sir?* 'Don't you see? Whereas if he came to, this afternoon...'

Steffie was looking on delightedly. 'Don't listen!' I said, covering her ears, and Sue began to laugh with me, and Steffie too. It was all too close to home.

'This is serious,' I said, and we broke up again.

'Jack, if you're really so sure...' said Sue, calming.

'I'm not. I'm not. Perhaps it isn't Bromley.'

The laughter had burst the bubble, made the sleuthing unreal.

'I bet it *is*,' came a voice from the kitchen. Claire appeared at Sue's shoulder. Sue moved aside, and she slipped into the sitting room. 'Of course it is,' repeated Claire, unsmiling. 'You know it is.' The laughter had gone.

'What do we do?'

'You ring,' said Claire. We all gazed at her as she sat down in an armchair, unruffled, taking her place in the audience. She was treating us as a teenager might treat tiresome parents who were squabbling again.

'Go on then,' Sue said.

I looked down at the pad, nervously. Claire was watching me. 'You do it,' I grinned. But they both gazed back, unrelenting. 'All right,' I said. I dialled, firmly, praying for a dead line. I listened, with three pairs of eyes on me. A click came, and a silence. There was someone there.

'Hello?' It was a voice used to subduing people. 'Laura Bromley here!'

The conversation went off far more easily than I'd expected. Laura Bromley had a wartime manner and the accent to go with it; and she didn't seem surprised that I was ringing from the blue. 'I'm an old pupil of John's,' I began, 'I wondered...' —Delighted! she barked, and took over. As I listened, Stefanie succumbed to giggles and had to be shushed by Claire. 'No, no, that's all right,' I said, 'it's just that I might be in your part of the world, so I was wondering—' I found myself in the throes of a hearty invitation. 'Yes, well I'd love to, yes.' I looked round at the waiting girls. 'I don't quite know.' I steeled myself. 'I see, yes. It's a funny thing, I thought I saw him in—on—sorry? No, I thought I saw John, you see, in Cromer. Cromer. Norfolk. On the pier there—just the other day.' Even Sue and Claire were now finding it hard to keep a straight face. 'In Norfolk, yes.' I waved a hand at them reproachfully. 'Right. Yes I will, and . . . give my regards to him. Yes. Jack Thurgo.' Come again? she bellowed. 'Well, Wilf Thurgo actually, Wilfred Thurgo. Officially. Just tell him Thurgo.' I had to wave angrily at the girls again; they were bent double. 'Goodbye, yes. Goodbye. Yes I will— goodbye!' By now I was bawling too. The ordeal over, I hung up.

Steffie broke the silence. 'Is that your real name?' she asked. I was still deep in thought.

'Yes,' I said, but so vaguely that everyone erupted. 'Yes of course it is,' I said, trying to quell the laughter.

'*Wilfred?*' Steffie spluttered.

'Wilf,' I nodded and, trying to regain the initiative: 'Wilf Sinda-combe.' The women laughed but Steffie now looked thoroughly confused—I'd have to explain it all to her in due course.

'Come on, Jack,' said Claire. 'Is he at home or not?'

'He isn't there,' I said. I was so pleased that Claire had used my name for the first time, that Sue's anger took me quite aback.

'Why didn't you *tell* her?' she threw at me.

'Because she knows where he is. He's in Aberdeen.'

'In *Aberdeen?*' Claire grinned, in disbelief.

I nodded. 'And she's heard from him.' But they saw my lame expression, and waited. 'A postcard,' I said.

'A *postcard?*' they echoed.

'Well?' I said. Nobody spoke. 'Anyway. She's expecting him back any day, for what that's worth.'

We contemplated this in silence.

'What's he doing in Aberdeen?' Sue asked.

'Judging a goat show,' I said without thinking twice, Laura Bromley's booming voice still in my head; the phone call had been too much of an ordeal to allow any accompanying reaction at all. Sue and Claire were rocking with laughter again. 'What's so funny now?' I asked defiantly. But the thought of the man snatching a dirty weekend by telling his wife he was judging a goat show was too much for me and I laughed helplessly along with them.

Once again our laughter robbed the situation of all urgency; and it exorcized the morning's anger. Sue went off to her friend Diana's, as planned. I never got lunch. Throughout my stay, for one reason or another, I failed to synchronize entirely with the Harding household. But it didn't matter. The Bromley business seemed to have brought me closer to Claire. And I knew this wasn't lost on Sue. She told Steffie to get ready to come to Diana's, but the child sulked. 'It's all right, we'll look after Stef,' I said; I didn't want to be so crudely stage-managed. Sue gave me a smiling look, and left.

The afternoon trickled away. We sat in the back garden, in the sun. Claire had an effortless elegance about her, even sprawled in the grass; I couldn't keep my eyes off her. Stefanie got fed up with her paints set and demanded to try proper water colours, so Claire brought down her own paints and the sketchbook. While she instructed Steffie, I leafed through the book. The sketches were limpid and graceful, and a little repetitive; she used a lot of water, and the effect was an attractive blur. They formed a sharp contrast to the painting in the sitting room, which was thickly luminous and in which everything except the human figures was geometric, all right angles and slanting shadow; there were no figures in these, not one. I remembered posing like a fool, the day before, while Claire sketched from the first floor window-seat. They were intriguing, they had atmosphere, but only one atmosphere, irrespective of time or place.

'These are lovely,' I said, leafing back through them. 'Only they're rather the same.'

'They're meant to be,' she said. 'It's one technique.' She smiled, and we left it at that.

I lay back and sunned myself. 'Are you going to go?' said Claire. 'Sorry?'

'To Wales,' she said. I looked at her, trying to gauge her concern. 'It did sound as though you were being invited.'

'I suppose so, yes. I didn't say when I was coming or anything. She was just being polite.' I dragged my mind back to Bromley. 'I don't know what he looks like, that's the trouble. Looks like now, I mean; it's been ten years. The school might have a photograph, I suppose.' A farewell snap. 'I bet they gave him quite a party when he left.' No Bromley; and a cheery chirpy girl's voice on the phone. Of course the place had changed, and now there was no going back, no sanctuary, I was locked towards the future.

Claire had turned back to the child. 'You can put a little water on, not too much, and let it run.' She showed her. I watched her slender fingers. 'You see?'

No-one could remove my picture of The Arbor. But now no-one could join me in it either.

'Can't I do it like this?' said Stefanie, daubing the colour on.

'Yes of course you can. Go ahead.'

Steffie worked in an orange sun. 'What does Jack do?' she said, as though I wasn't there.

'Ask him.'

She didn't.

'I'm a bookseller,' I said grandly.

'He works in Mummy's bookshop,' Claire explained.

Stefanie eyed me for a time. Then she leaned over to Claire and whispered in her ear. I couldn't catch it. Claire glanced up at me and grinned. 'No need to whisper,' she said to the child, who was sitting back waiting for an answer. Steffie leaned forward and whispered again. Claire looked down, smiling, and poured some water on the orange sun. 'What does that mean, her boyfriend?'

'*What?*' I said.

'*Is* he?' exulted Stefanie.

'No of course not,' Claire said.

'Yes he is.'

'How do you know?' Claire grinned at her. Neither of them looked at me.

'Did she tell you?' Steffie asked Claire.

'No.'

'Why is it a secret?'

'It's not.'

'Now hold on...' I said.

'I don't think she's going to tell me,' said the child.

'Yes she will.'

'No she won't, she'll pretend nothing's going on.'

Steffie went back to her painting, smearing gold along the skyline. I smiled at Claire, trying to retrieve my position, but she was watching the child paint. 'Look,' said Stefanie, and glanced up at her.

'Yes, that's nice.' And in the same tone, 'She probably doesn't want to upset you.'

'I'm not upset, I'd just like her to explain to me.'

'Explain what?' Claire said. I seemed to have no part in this. 'I think Mummy likes a cuddle now and again,' Claire said gently. 'Don't you think?'

'Yes,' said Steffie, and worked brightly at the paper.

'Good. Then you understand.' Claire looked at me at last, conspiratorial.

'Yes,' said Steffie. 'Like Bromley.' She studied the painting. 'Look. I've made a rotten horrible mess.'

'Yes,' said Claire, and mixed some paint. 'Now we'll try it my way.'

SUE FAILED TO show up for supper. Claire didn't seem very

surprised. The evening stretched ahead of us; babysitting. As she put Stefanie to bed, I stared at myself in the mirror of the downstairs loo. Girly features; sometimes I wanted to mutilate them. And my hair was sticking up. 'Here, didn't I cut yours two weeks ago?' the barber said; I'd just met Chrissie at the time. 'You courting, are you?' 'Sorry?' 'Well, your hair grows faster when you're courting.' I slicked my hair down with a little water and went back into the sitting room.

I put on some classical music and sat on the sofa, waiting. I had little experience at this. Chrissie and I had courted, that first week, to Mozart on her record player. 'Be sociable...' I kept saying, as I edged across the bedspread in her digs. I was eighteen; when Chrissie turned sociable, I spoke of love; I couldn't find a way of putting the other, *love or lust, boy,* into words. I'd never really had occasion to separate the two, and at school we were starved of both.

Footsteps coming lightly down the stairs. Claire smiled at me as she entered to the music. 'That's nice.'

'Oh good,' I said. She swung on through into the kitchen. I followed. 'No sign of Sue.'

'She won't be back till late. Diana's is a sort of refuge.'

'Is she all right?' I asked.

Claire smiled. 'You're asking *me?*' She was unnervingly assured.

I nodded. 'I haven't seen her for almost six months, not since she bought this place. She never comes round the bookshop any more.'

'They've been doing an awful lot of decorating here,' Claire said. We washed up together.

David, talking about writing books, putting up shelves instead. I asked Claire how she got on with him. She shrugged coolly, non-committal. I wasn't too surprised. Chrissie claimed to detest him; once, on a London visit, he had described to her the night he'd just spent with a Dutch girl, 'expert at kissyface' as he put it. In bed it had been all Masters and Johnson, acrobatics, he complained. 'You should be grateful,' Chrissie had admonished him. 'I don't fuck the ladies for their pleasure,' David said, 'I fuck to save my soul.' My wellbred English soul recoiled when Chrissie told me this; but I knew what David meant, I'd read about it in Norman Mailer, under his guidance. Chrissie never forgave him. There were just two kinds of people in her book, givers and takers, and she knew which he was. I told David she thought he was a taker. 'What do *you* think?' he said. I had my answer pat. 'I think there are two kinds of people,' I said, 'those who think there are two kinds of people, and those who don't.'

He loved me: I was avid for his talk, his confidence, and his refusal to settle for anything less than the miraculous, than salvation. I loved to watch his grace and care as he rebuilt the Suffolk piggery, each crooked beam, each slate posing a question to the infinite. Though like Sue he couldn't resist a dash of American whimsy, a tobacco tin or an empty pill-bottle wedged into the cement. We stood and looked at the work from every angle; David talked of Jansenism and the hero, who never ceases to seek God and only lives in order to seek Him; who knows the impossibility of finding God and realizing any value, and who knows he is intrinsically guilty in the eyes of the deity who sees all and demands nothing less than the miracle. I was uneasy about all this guilt, Chrissie was always feeling guilty, I was guilty, everyone was guilty. David believed in the Fall, the 'fault against the essence'. We heaved another rafter into place. He built, he said, like the Elizabethans, 'to the end of the beam': if his chosen beam stuck out past the end of the house, it stuck out, never mind the geometry. I was always producing gloomy calcula-tions. But despite my predictions and Sue's, the piggery never fell down. David, however, did. His fall was more a fault against common sense than against the essence; working alone in a high wind one afternoon, something he'd warned me never to do, he tumbled from the roof and cracked a vertebra. Unaided, he crawled back to the house, four hours he said it took. Then he crawled back again and fed the pigs. He loved a crisis. The grass, he swore, was watching. When his neighbour's business failed and the man hanged himself, David took on both farms, and the neighbour's family, till they recovered. They worshipped him, though as Sue pointed out, they didn't have to live with him. In fact I rather suspected the wife did live with him; but she soon sold the farm and left the district. 'He's awfully good with Stefanie,' I said to Claire, 'whenever I've seen them together.' She nodded. It was undeniable; Stefanie followed him around; they spoke a secret language, swineherd talk. 'Oop shooby,' they murmured, in the rustling piggery, a quiet scat song. 'Oooby shoobs.' But Claire was obviously less impressed. David's confidences flattered me—'tis thee and me, he would say, against the godless hordes—but I was maddened and offended by his dogmatism, and a little scared of his reproof; it was reassuring to hear someone else run him down, while I stood up for him alone, judiciously. 'Does Sue still want a child with him, d'you think?' I said. Claire dried her hands over the sink, without looking at me. Then she folded the dishcloth and made briskly for the sitting room.

'Steffie can hear every word we say,' she said as she went, pointing at the floor above, and the child's bedroom.

'In here too?' I asked, following her.

'No.'

She sat in an armchair and I went back to the sofa. We listened to the music for a while, and Claire gave me a long appraising look. I felt the subject stood a second shot: 'D'you think they'll ever have one?' I said. But Claire only smiled faintly, in polite acknowledgement, as if to show it was none of her business. I talked, to cover the awkwardness, and to encourage Claire. 'I think David has his reasons,' I said, 'in this day and age. For not wanting a child.' Claire gazed at me. To beget the Christ child, David had said, that was the sole purpose of procreation. 'On the other hand,' I went on, 'he does admit to a feeling of nausea, actual nausea, when he thinks of fatherhood. Which doesn't seem to have too much to do with overpopulation and so forth . . . why are you looking at me like that?'

'Like what?' After a moment she gave in, grinning. 'If you really want to know, I was thinking that, well,' the grin broadened, 'he doesn't really need a son. Not if he's got you.'

'Well I don't know, he doesn't *treat* me like a son.' Under her gaze I wondered what I meant: how *did* a father treat a son? 'The thing is, I wonder if he isn't afraid of losing Sue—being supplanted in her interest. I mean, Steffie's only here part of the year.' I paused. 'I don't think I'd feel that way myself, really.'

'I don't know what she sees in him,' said Claire.

It was the wrong tack, clearly. 'Her singing seems to be going a treat,' I said. Claire looked down at her hands. I looked out of the window, at the garden, and thought about a move. Perhaps moonlight would do the trick.

She was eyeing me once again. 'I suppose you know Sue's seeing a psychiatrist.'

'No,' I said, startled. 'I didn't know.' I was about to ask Claire whether she held David responsible for this state of affairs, when I saw she was starting to smile. I held back, puzzled.

The smile grew. 'I don't think David approves. Sue says she's having fun. It's given her a few ideas.'

'Really? What sort of ideas?'

'Don't you know?' she said, and giggled. 'It's a woman, the psychiatrist, I mean. She told Sue she ought to have an affair.'

'I didn't think psychiatrists did things like that,' I said. 'Are you sure?' Claire nodded, and bit her lip. Her eyes teased. The message was clear, and suddenly I understood why the going had been so sticky.

'Look,' I said, 'it was David who invited me down here. Not Sue.'

'Was it?'

'I'm not having an affair with her.'

'Of course you're not.'

Of course you're not. Sarcasm; or . . . then the penny dropped. 'Are *you*?'

She stared at me. 'No.' She seemed genuinely shocked.

'I'm glad to hear it.' I could see her starting—I thought—to reconsider her assumption about Sue and me. 'But would you tell me, if you were?'

'Don't be so silly,' she said, and shifted on the armchair. 'I feel like a drink. Do you?' I fumbled in the cupboards, feigning ignorance until she came and helped me out, finding the glasses. I took my Scotch and positioned myself between Claire and the unbreachable armchair. We stood.

'What kind of music did you play? Your band?' she asked. The classical record had given out. I tootled my Funny Valentine solo, Chet Baker style, complete with record-stuck-in-the-groove effect, till Claire eased back grinning onto the sofa. Better. 'What happened there?' she giggled. 'That was where the record I was learning from got stuck,' I said. 'I was a slow learner. I played it so often it got scratched to hell and gone. I never did learn how it finished.' We subsided. 'Who *is* Sue having an affair with, then?' I said, as I sat beside her. She shrugged in ignorance, smiling. I mused. 'The psychiatrist?'

'You're obsessed.' She made it sound friendly. 'Sue doesn't want to go to bed with me. We're friends, that's all.'

'Exactly,' I said. Her hand was close beside me. I was floating, at the thought of touching it. 'And you and I?' I said. Be sociable. I looked down at her fingers. 'Are we going to be friends?'

'I hope so.'

I took the hand. 'You've got the loveliest hands,' I said. 'And breasts.'

Claire eyed me sideways. 'Small but quality,' she said firmly, nodding. I grinned, closed in, and she yielded demurely to the kiss.

'Short but quality,' I said. And clarified hastily, 'The kiss, I mean.'

'Of course,' she said. 'What else?' She took back her hand to pick up the drink.

I sat back. 'What got into Sue this morning?' I said. No need to

hurry now. 'Steffie's all right.' There was a pause. 'Isn't she?'
Claire gazed at her drink. 'How much longer is she staying?'

'Another month.'

'And you?' I touched the curve of her shoulder, watched her now
familiar mouth, possessively.

'I'll stay until she leaves.' Claire sipped her drink, conscious of my
gaze. 'You've got a girlfriend,' she said. 'Sue told me.'

'True,' I said. 'You've got a feller.' She nodded. 'In London,' I
said, and went on playing with her shoulder. She didn't stop me, and
I put my arm around her.

'Sue might come back,' she said, 'any time now.'

'That's not what you said earlier.' She wasn't looking at me.
'Besides, I don't think she's . . . opposed to this,' I said. Claire gave
a quizzical sort of frown. 'In fact she let slip that you weren't wholly
averse to me,' I grinned, knowing I was taking a wrong turn.

'She *what?*' said Claire and eyed me sharply. Then to my surprise
she gave a snort, amused, and grinned down at her glass. 'When did
she say this?'

'Oh. Earlier. Today.'

Claire nodded. 'Well, I think she misunderstood,' she said, and
laughed. I studied her, put out.

'Really?'

'Last night, when I came in, we had a talk, Sue and I. Well, *she*
started to talk. I was dead beat, but she wanted to talk about her
psychiatrist woman.' Claire grinned at me and hesitated. I nodded.
'All right . . .' she said. 'Sue asked me whether I thought you were
attractive. I thought she was asking with, you know, herself in mind.
Not me. She's just been telling me how this psychiatrist had told her
to have an affair, so I mean . . . anyway, I said yes, I did think you
were attractive. So as not to be rude.' Claire laughed again.

'Oh I see,' I said. She was still chortling.

'Not that I don't think you're attractive.'

'Oh good.' I waited for her to settle.

She looked me over. 'You must admit it's funny.'

'Well, as long as the laugh's on Sue,' I said, and stood up, smiling. 'More soft music?' She nodded and I went and fiddled with the record player.

Claire sat with her back to me. 'I'm not going to sleep with you,' she said abruptly, and with a dry edge I hadn't heard before.

'No need to decide now,' I said. 'Wait till you've heard my next solo.' I put the record on the turntable, my fingers shaking. I came back to the sofa and sat looking at her, but she met my gaze all too easily, and shook her head. She let me take her hand; the electricity had gone.

'Because of your feller?' I said. She didn't answer. 'He's in London.'

'He comes down.'

'What's he do?' I asked. She shrugged, as though there was no answer. 'I've known him since school. He does a lot of sport, mainly.'

I interlocked our fingers.

'Don't, Jack,' she said, 'I mustn't.' Her gaze was friendly, and final. A great relief surged through me. I gave a brave smile, bent and gathered up her glass.

'You understand, don't you?' Claire asked.

I nodded solemnly.

'Then you're the only one round here who does,' she said.

I MADE NO more advances. It was a moral victory, I told myself; and on the other hand, in my restraint, I was a hero, perhaps *the* hero, though I didn't feel as David did, with Pascal, intrinsically guilty. I knew I was at fault, of course. Doubtless against the essence. But what had Bromley said? Women have no moral character? What an old liar he was.

I lay in bed and thought of Claire, wraith-like beneath the sheets, in the room next to mine. Was she awake? There was no sound. Outside the window a mechanical belfry tolled the hours. I got up and took book after book from David's shelves, books on myth, *Myths Rediscovered*, *Myths Of The World*, myths of every sort, I even tried David's own early book of essays, *Aping God*, based on his fieldwork in Indonesia; but I couldn't get through more than a few pages before the lines blurred and I was reading them again. In the end I went back to bed. I thought of everyone but Chrissie; everything bar marriage. Thought of The Arbor; Bromley days; my private bolt-hole. Running for Malta through laurel and yew—but all that was long gone now, our cocoon of postwar relief and coronation glee, with Bromley standing guard over the books of the dead. All gone. And now an old feeling began to stalk me. I wanted to bring it on, I always did. The first bout had occurred there in the army hut, a heavily cladded prefab which had functioned as our sick bay, the school 'san'. There were always half a dozen of us in there, on and off, during the winter term. It was night, I was breathing asthmatically, trying to control my panic, when something separate from the struggle to breathe began to rise in me, something more troubling. I couldn't identify it. Later I didn't need bronchitis, I could bring the feeling on at will, but I still couldn't find a name for it. For a short time, at public school, the name rang loud and clear: nostalgia. I felt a choking need to be back at The Arbor, to walk through the front gates, under the chestnut trees, to glimpse the school rooms, to go down along the railway line, unseen, to the pavilion. I was unhappy, that was all. The longing passed, soon enough, but over the years the panic, the suffocation terror, kept returning. I was a forgotten miner, trapped beneath the ground; a lost earthquake survivor; a hero from Edgar Allan Poe, waking in the coffin. I tried the name of death—was that it? No, not death, not pain, not even nothingness; rather the waiting, time itself; though I wasn't waiting, I provoked these crises, summoned them, summoned something too vast to be the shudder of a finite soul before eternity.

76

It felt as if it would explode me. It was more like eternity itself aghast at numbers.

In the school san that first time I'd struggled to lie still. But it was too much for me and I slid out to pace the walkway in between the rows of sleeping, wheezing boys. Now the need was to leave the hut. I could already picture myself running aimlessly, then, by extension, on a train in my pyjamas, hurtling somewhere. It wasn't a voice calling me, nothing beckoned beyond the door, no moon drew me, no lunacy. Only the need to outrun my billowing terror, by running straight into the tunnel: into it. I walked the grounds that night in my bare feet, in my dressing gown. Nobody saw me.

I'd never given in since then, never that far. Never beyond a corridor, outside a room. There was no point: there was nothing beyond, and I knew it. Outside was always The Arbor, the moonlit grounds circled by beech trees and bracken. I'd calm myself and go back to the room. And afterwards the relief was all-obliterating, I was back from outer space. It brought the taste of nectar, dearly bought. The foreground surged towards me, tactile: I was home.

But I was far from home, in David's study. I sat, rigid, in his bed, summoning the void—a second Crowley. Why didn't I quell the terror, put it back on the shelf? I always knew I could. At that moment I pictured myself: no, not Crowley, I was Bomber Bromley, staring Bromley, amimic in the hospital bed, sitting up in borrowed pyjamas. I felt the panic yield before my laughter.

I would not be spooked by Bromley; Bromley was ill. Amimia, Paratonia. See Oculogyria. It sounded like one of those mythical islands in David's books, from which no mariner returned. See Oculogyria and die.

The corridor was dark and still, I went out easily, cheerfully, before need drove me to it. This way I was a step ahead. Halfway down the stairs I had to slow up, shaky. When I reached the sitting room I put the light on and stood in the doorway, gazing at the furniture. It wasn't over yet. I needed a witness; the room was unnervingly foreign. Where was the face I had to see? I'd outstared death as best I could. What, then? The future held no fears, it was banal. Recorded time was far more terrifying, but there was no moment I wanted to return to—not any more—and nothing I would have changed. I went to break the silence, to the record player, and put on the piece I'd chosen, blind, for Claire. Schubert. It was a mistake, a frightening one. Time yawed, as if the record had warped in the night. I couldn't catch a melody; I concentrated, gripping the record player in both hands. The music sloughed as if in a gusty wind, brought nausea, Schubert in broken time. I pulled the needle up and off and turned back to the room.

It was a funfair crazy-house, with a berserk geometry built to the end of some warped mental beam. Only the painting, with its escaping figures, held still. They had their backs to me. They wouldn't, couldn't leave the frame, and I willed them to stay. I willed them to stay in the room.

'You haven't stayed up for me?'

Sue was in the doorway. Her voice undulated like the music: the spell wasn't broken yet. I needed to blurt out something, some word; not Chrissie; what? This is what it's like, then, I thought. Going mad, buried alive in your body. Sue took me to the sofa, sat me down. I must have been staring at her. 'Say something,' she was saying.

'I'm all right. I couldn't sleep.' Release came over me like a sweat, at the sound of my own voice. I glanced up at the painting. They were all there, the man with the two children, the housewife disappearing down the street, the unforgiving onlooker above the windowbox with its silly flowers, pink, perhaps geraniums.

I looked down and realized I wasn't wearing anything.

I stood up, 'Must put something on.'

'Don't be stupid.'

Sue pulled me gently back onto the sofa, held my hands. 'What's the matter?'

'Just dizzy.'

She studied me. 'I didn't think I'd find you up,' she smiled, teasing. 'Alone.'

'Ah well,' I said. 'I did my best.'

She eyed me, still smiling. 'You mustn't get so upset.'

'No, not about that,' I assured her. 'Really not.' I could hear my voice holding a normal conversation.

We were looking at each other, and I leant across and hugged her, my face in her black velvet jacket. For a time we held each other tight. But I was all right again, and I began to feel uneasy, naked against her clothes. 'What's that painting?' I asked, without looking. 'Claire said it was French.' Sue let me go, and stood up. She went over to it.

'Yes,' she said. 'He was a Paris postman, the painter.' She studied the signature. 'Rimbert. He's in his seventies now.' She lifted the frame off the wall. I had a resurgence of anxiety; but the painting left no mark behind it, no mocking frame of dust. It was a newly decorated room. 'He's been called the Primitives' Vermeer,' said Sue with satisfaction.

She put the painting in my lap. It was small, some fifteen inches square, and covered me conveniently. 'You like it?' she said.

I nodded. On the canvas, the light slanted across the little street beyond the doorway. The tones were gold and brown and parchment yellow, in heavy, sticky paint, paint to which I'd felt, moments before, that I owed my sanity; now this seemed absurd.

'I'd like you to have it,' Sue smiled down at me.

'No,' I said, and took it over to the wall.

'Please, Jack. There's other things we can put in its place.'

I didn't know how to explain. I needed it on the wall. I shook my head and steadied it in place, then crossed, embarrassed, to switch off the silent record player. 'I'm off to bed.' Sue watched my naked parade.

'There's something wrong. What is it?'

'Nothing really. Claustrophobia, sort of.'

She paused. 'D'you want a pill? A sleeping pill?'

I nodded. It would get us out.

'Don't go,' she said. 'Tell me about it.' I stood, saying nothing, afraid to cry. 'You could sleep down here,' she said gently.

'It's not the room.'

I felt pressure building again, inside, and I quashed it without moving. Outside, The Arbor and the grounds. Sue came and took me by the hand. We sat once more.

'There's someone you could see,' she said, 'if you felt like it.' I said nothing. 'A therapist. You'd like her. I sent David to her.' Sue smiled and I smiled with her. 'I don't know what he said to her,' she grinned, 'but she didn't want to see him any more, she wanted to see me.'

'Lady pyschiatrist?' I feigned ignorance. 'He probably scared the daylights out of her.'

'I doubt it; she likes crazy people. And I've been going ever since. Not a psychiatrist: a therapist. And it's not at all what I expected—to begin with, she's *the* most beautiful woman.'

'And you send David to her?'

'Oh, she's good, she shakes you up. I went thinking she might have one or two ideas. She says her patients always think she's there to bring the glad news. That's why they need help.' Sue gazed at me. 'She said I didn't need her at all. Sin and repent, that's my advice to you. Go out and sin and you'll feel better.'

I smiled uncertainly. 'But you've been going back to her.'

'I haven't sinned, is all.' She squeezed my hand. A moment passed. 'Anyhow: I said, look, all I want is a friend. I just want a friend.' Sue paused. 'She said, that's all right, find a friend, and then you won't need *me*.' There was a silence. 'One thing she said,' Sue's gaze slipped off me, '—that we all want to be members of the chorus. Equal and unenvying, like angels. We want to be friends.'

She made it sound impossible. Besides, hadn't there been a certain amount of jostling in the angelic choirs, beginning with Lucifer himself? I noticed Sue drawing herself up, erect: the lady therapist.

'And what we want, my dear Sue,' she mimicked, 'we shall have.' With the accent it was more like Mrs Langley. Sue glanced at me.

'All dreams are prophetic, that what she says. *All* dreams.'

There was a twist to her expression. Speaking was difficult.

'Would you mind if I went off for a couple of days?' I said.

Sue looked at me, raised my hands in hers, then let them fall. 'I guess not,' she said, finally. Then she grinned broadly at me. 'No, of course not.'

'Have you got an atlas?' I said.

THE MAN IN the cottage hospital was going to be transferred to Norwich General for observation and some sort of liquid feeding machine. There was no change in his condition. No sign of Mrs Sindacombe either, despite a radio alert. This I was told by Mrs Stevenson in mid-morning. I put the phone down and made my way dozily into the kitchen; I felt rough, Sue's sleeping pill had knocked me out. I'd missed breakfast again.

Before passing out, in the early hours, I'd sat in bed over the maps, computing distances. The Black Mountains strode threateningly down the page: two hundred and fifty miles of cycling, all told, to Builth Wells and Bromley's retirement bungalow. In my hallucinatory state it looked like an adventure. In the morning I gazed sluggishly down from the window at my bicycle. One day's exercise tended to quench the summer's need. I was a train, hurtling into a tunnel; that was the Metaphor. After coffee I got Sue to drive me to the station halt at Sheringham.

That morning several postcards had arrived, mine a view of the Chicago stockyards in the old days. *Jackson banana*, it read, *America is losing its bedoobies. The young want to be Indians and the old want to run Little Big Horn again, this time with howitzers. Chicago still bellows but it's all mechanical steers now. This dying buffalo can't find a butcher man.* There was no mention of job prospects. I glanced at Sue as we raced down the coast road in the Vitesse. 'He *is* coming back,' I said. 'Isn't he?'

'Oh sure,' she said.

We said nothing about the night before. Sue was preoccupied; there was nothing in her postcard either, about the job. The way she drove, I thought it was my last journey, but it woke me up. A grotesque old hotel leered down at us as we sped through Shering-ham, long grasses sprouting from its turrets and obscuring the mansard windows. A dusty two-compartment train waited, by the tiny stretch of tarmac where British Rail had improvised a terminus. The old station beside it, it turned out, was a museum.

'Regards to Bromley,' Sue smiled confidently, as I climbed out of the car.

'We'll see,' I said.

She pulled me back into the open window for a motherly kiss. 'Come back soon.' I nodded. She was wearing an improbable perfume.

The train smelt like an ashtray; as it pulled forwards I felt the familiar freedom, no more heeby-jeebs as David called them, no more *angor animi*. I was home again. I had borrowed David's rucksack for the journey, replete with stickers from an earlier road culture. Pasadena, here I come.

At Birmingham the guard shook me awake. It was night, and the train was empty and still, I'd got into it at Norwich in mid-afternoon, and somewhere in the trailing conurbation between Coventry and Birmingham I'd dozed off. New Street station was deserted. Shouldering my pack I crossed the road into a maze of precinct architecture, underpasses, ringway roads. Some hardy souls, or drunks, lay with their legs tucked under them, in passageways, asleep. I surfaced to a small oasis of old streets circled by flyovers. A neon sign beckoned.

Small hotels only reminded me of Chrissie, of holidays we'd taken on the continent, of nights in drab and undemanding rooms, of making love.

'All right, dear?' said the girl on night duty, pushing the door wide to reveal my room. She was a fat blonde woman, taller than I was, the flesh bulging out of her clothes, but her voice was weak and thin as though exhausted by her body.

'Perfect,' I said.

Chrissie and I had gone abroad to France on two occasions, and once to her beloved Italy. In Perugia we had been obliged to take a room with six beds—it was, they said, the only one left in the hotel so they'd let us have it cheap. I swore to baptize each bed in turn, though we finally settled for less, rumpling the remaining ones to give a sporting impression of the British sex drive. From there I took Chrissie—it made a change from the museums and cathedrals she showed me—to review the Bromley battlefield at Montepulciano. I had a great desire, that summer, to cycle over the Alps: there was a modest pass above Turin that could be managed in a day. Old bicycles were easy to find now that Vespa and Lambretta were taking over, but I couldn't persuade Chrissie to join me. I left her to take the train, and cheated the ascent by hanging onto the back of a heavy lorry for the best part of the climb up to the pass. Then freewheeled into Barcelonette, ticking off the kilometres, through Sisteron and Gap, towards Chrissie, dreaming of our reunion. Those too were golden times. We met in Avignon; more churches, castles, more hotel rooms. In the prehistoric museum at Les Eyzies we had a famous row. It was, predictably, about her mother. We were both tired after a night in a rat-infested barn. The whole thing had really begun the day before, when Chrissie with her usual effrontery decided to visit a man she scarcely knew, in a grand house on the Auvézère. She didn't actually know him at all, except by repute. He was a poet she admired, a middle-aged Frenchman; and she'd got his address from one of her professors, though she didn't tell me this until we reached the area. Chrissie said all she wanted was a bath. But I knew better. And I felt sure from the look of the place that the man didn't want sweaty hitchhikers from England rocking up on the lawn. Chrissie was not to be deterred. Even at home she queue-barged with a tourist's gall, so much so that I'd sometimes been left to catch the bus behind hers, after hanging back in sheer embarrassment at her behaviour. She strode up to the poet's gates, while I prayed he was out. He wasn't. A tiny, hawklike man came to the door and smiled at us. It was too beautiful a day to set the dogs on anyone, and I knew from his expression we were in. As I might have guessed, he was entranced by Chrissie's forwardness. She was so brash, dark-eyed and dark-complexioned, smiling sexuality. Her French was perfect. I was on a losing wicket from the start. She got her bath; I knew she was courting a further invitation. Monsieur Jacot showed me politely round the grounds, spaniels snuffling at our heels, as we waited for *mademoiselle*. He was reserved, and diffidently offered lunch, but in my jealousy I suspected his motives and, as we toured the sumptuous gardens, his poetic dedication. Then, as he pointed out the wistaria planted by his grandfather—an aristocrat by the sound of it, which at least explained the château—I felt his hand at my elbow, and the discreet pressure brought home to me that it was I, if anyone, who would receive the further invitation. After lunch I insisted we move on, to Chrissie's fury; the hotels proved to be full; and we ended up among the rats, in some foul-smelling barn.

In the museum Chrissie's anger spilled over. Our post-mortem on the *affaire Jacot* centred on what Chrissie termed my fantasy that he was going to make a pass at me. 'You see it everywhere,' she said. I gestured in vindication: all around us stone age bison, bear, and antelope coupled, like with like, on the museum walls. She saw my story as a plain lie, to disguise my jealousy, both erotic and intel-lectual. Her mother had a story about Chrissie's youthful innocence with regard to homosexuals, and I made the mistake of quoting it. Chrissie rounded on me. You and my mother, she began, and made some primitive suggestions; luckily we were alone. I loved her mother. I had a theory that you couldn't love the daughter without loving the mother. Tenderly, of course. I'd even mentioned it to Mrs Wolfe. I knew she loved me like a son. But Chrissie was obsessed with the idea that her mother had extinguished her, Chrissie's, true vocation: an exercise book full of early adolescent verse had been mocked to death, she claimed. It seemed a poor excuse. Behind it all lay the family tragedy. Chrissie's elder sister, a ferociously bright and neurotic girl, had gassed herself, between university terms. I knew Chrissie laid this at her mother's door, with the time-honoured charge of crushing ambition forced on the children. But the girl I knew had forced herself too hard without encouragement. It was all nonsense. It was Chrissie's permanent excuse, but my views were disqualified, of course: I didn't know Jewish families. They were different. They were different from my own, I knew that, but they weren't so far removed from many gentile families I'd met. The Jewish problem, as I came across it with Chrissie, began with the fact that they were different. They affirmed it constantly. But if anyone else said so, it was a genocidal slur. They were misunderstood; but whose was the misunderstanding? Perhaps they weren't actually so different after all.

That night, in the Birmingham hotel, I dreamt about her family. It was a pleasant dream. We sat around the dinner table. I was fussed over; I was the honoured guest. When I looked up at Mr Wolfe's place at the head of the table, David stood there instead. He smiled proudly. 'As Freddie Hegel used to say,' he began in his deep voice, raising his knife over the Sunday joint, 'come, children! Let us fulfil its destiny!'

This sliver of dream came back to me in the morning as I sat in the breakfast room, waiting for my fry-up. Commercial travellers sat numbly at their places round the room. They watched as my plate was brought in; tomato, egg, bread, sausage, and grease. None of them looked appetizing enough to eat. I turned to my book, to finish the page.

It was a wonderful morning, and the Master was walking home, I read. The eternal Sufi Master, always on top of adversity. Which of the slimy objects on my plate would he have recommended starting with? *Why, he thought to himself, should he not take a short cut through the woodland beside the dusty road?* Why indeed. *A day of days, a day of fortunate pursuits! he exclaimed to himself, plunging into the greenery. Almost at once, he found himself at the bottom of a concealed pit.*

'Kippers, or the fry?' The blowsy woman was asking my next door neighbour, a nice-looking fellow in a suit. The other guests minded their own business in silence. My neighbour took a furtive look at my plate. I kept a straight face.

'Kippers,' he said faintly. As the woman left, he and I exchanged a polite smile. I turned back to the Master.

It is just as well I took this short cut, the Master reflected as he lay there, because if a thing like this can happen in the midst of such beauty, what catastrophe might not have developed on that uncompromisingly tiresome highway?

I marked the page, and ate.

BEHIND BUILTH WELLS I followed a Welsh Avon to the mountains, hilltops bald and beautiful above trim valley fields. I was still relieved I hadn't brought the bike. The sun shone hard out of a cloudless sky as I toiled up the hill towards Gwaun village. The new bungalow, Mrs Bromley had said; the village shopkeeper knew it at once. Gwaun was all stone and slate. The Colt house, he said, wooden slats, brown. Goats. He pointed me further up the mountain and I climbed on past some deserted summer cottages, into rough pasture. Beside an electrified fence I said good morning to a mouse-grey goat, which stared at me, chomping, across the wire. I paused for breath, and for thought. The Colt house was visible, harsh in its glinting, varnished weatherboarding, brown beneath the gritty fabric roofing. A broad-shouldered figure, a woman, stooped in the front garden.

I walked slowly up the track towards her. The pack felt heavy. The woman was weeding energetically, without looking up. I stopped a little way off, and turned to the view. The river wound unseen beneath the dense trees in the valley; there were two landscapes, the cosy fields and cottages, bound by hedgerows, and the stark domes of fading grass, unfenced, above the tree line. 'Good morning,' came a voice.

'Morning,' I called, turning back. She was standing now, over the flowerbeds. A stout fence protected them from the solitary goat.

'Beautiful, isn't it. A beautiful morning,' she cried.

'Yes. It's glorious.' I walked towards the fence. What would I say? Here was a woman contentedly gardening, waiting for her husband to return from a trip to Scotland, and I was going to tell her that he was actually lying comatose at the other end of the country, under a false name. Or rather that someone was who looked uncannily like him. Which wouldn't ease her mind at all. I was wavering. Then too, in my mind's eye, Bromley came round the corner of the narrow Norfolk lane, with his hand outstretched. Bromley's eyes pleading: don't let on! . . . But a voice within me pointed out that this was hopelessly far-fetched—the man was just bewildered, dazed, looking for help. Pull yourself together, boy. 'You wouldn't be Mrs Bromley, would you?' I said.

'I would,' she said, ringingly. 'And who might you be?'

'Jack. Jack Thurgo.'

'Thurgo.' She looked me up and down. Her face cleared. 'Did you ring us?'

'That's right.'

'But my dear boy, why didn't you phone today? I could have come and fetched you. Come on in.' She stripped off rubber gloves. 'I told Johnny you'd phoned. He was absolutely thrilled.'

She headed for the house. I stared after her, trying to take this in, but hampered by the novel sense of Bromley as a Johnny.

'He's at home?' I said, unsteadily. But she was stamping her gumboots on the concrete path to the front door.

As I followed her, she disappeared into the house, calling. I lifted off the backpack and set it beside the door. The brown slats of the walls looked friendlier from close to, and the house smelt warm and woody in the sun. Mrs Bromley appeared in the doorway, frowning mutely at me, with a sort of puzzled belligerence, as though I had just caused her husband to disappear. She stood there for a moment, then plunged off around the building without a word. I left the pack and hurried after her.

'Johnny? Johnny?' she called. I felt pins and needles in my hands. 'Where is the silly old bugger?' she said abruptly.

A door opened in answer, and we turned. There was a building at the back, obscured by the main house. An army hut; for an instant I was staring at the school 'san'; as if he'd brought it, ailing boys and all, to Wales. A man emerged into the sunshine.

'I'm here,' said Bromley.

His face wore a cheerful grimace, a bit abstracted. He squinted against the light and came towards me, wiping his hands on his jacket. If my expression looked peculiar, he didn't seem to notice. For a moment—only an instant but a heart-stopping one—I thought I was seeing a completely different man, as though I'd so utterly misremembered Bromley that he bore no resemblance at all to the man I'd mistaken for him, and I was so alarmed by this possibility as it occurred to me (without knowing if it came from inside me or from what I was seeing) that I literally couldn't see the face in front of me, the face of Bromley, at all. Then sanity returned in a rush, as I gaped at him. It *was* the same man I'd been studying in the hospital bed. The hair was all awry, the clothes were dirty. But it *was*—it was the same face, the same build, the same man. Yes, and this was precisely what had sent my subconscious into shock. More rational than I, my mind had been expecting a different face, since, after all, this was impossible—how *could* it be the same man?

'It's Jack,' prompted Mrs Bromley brightly. 'He's just arrived.'

'Jack. My dear fellow.'

I was speechless. Bromley put out his hand. The outstretched hand: it seemed like a signal between us. But his face showed no more than normal cordiality. I took his hand, unnerved. He held mine in a casual grip, the same dry grip. Now there was something struggling in his gaze. It seemed to be embarrassment. I couldn't hold his eyes, I glanced down at his hands, the dirty nails.

'My d-dear chap,' he said. The faint stammer; I looked back at his face and saw a forced affability. I realized. The eyes told me: he hadn't the faintest idea who I was.

'I'll put the kettle on, shall I?' said Laura who had seen it too and came to the rescue with a hint. 'Old students deserve a cup of tea.' I left the answer to Bromley, but he was still clasping my hand, his smile now even more anxious and intent. Mrs Bromley turned to me. 'Or would you like ... something to eat...'

'Go ahead. You carry on,' said Bromley, and released me. 'I'll just fa-finish in here. Feeding the beasts.'

'Can I give you a hand?' I said. He glanced at Laura, then at me. I tried to read the message in his eyes. He seemed to straighten up, and nodded, firmly.

'Yes, come along,' he said. 'I'll introduce you. What it is, you see, I'm halfway round. The others will go mad if I don't feed them too. They're great jumpers, goats, they'll be in our front room if they're not satisfied.'

We climbed the steps towards the hut door—the school 'san' door—it was *identical*, dizzying—the familiar pre-fab walls, the cladding, the pale green door, the same paint—

'Dreadfully keen on their rights. I have to milk them in the same order each day, you know. Or else they eat my hair.'

The rush of talk, to cover his embarrassment; I wasn't fooled. He knew who I was. I could sense the coming game. At the door, I took a breath. Instead of the sharp smell of cleaning fluid, a warm stench. We penetrated the dark hut. At first I could see nothing. Bromley turned back and shut the door laboriously, making it darker still. A dustbin lid clanged, and I heard a rustling sound of grain. In the shadows along the hut walls I made out two rows of motionless heads. Where beds had been, the stalls ranged, tall enough to hide all but each goat's expectant face, turned to the noise of food. Bromley came past me, carrying a metal scoop, and stood gazing at his charges. I knew the pose.

There was a classroom silence as the goats watched us in return. 'Good of you to come, boy,' he said. I couldn't see his expression.

HE FED THE goats in turn, without a word. They dug their faces into plastic buckets, eating greedily. I slowly grew accustomed to the half-light, watching them. I wasn't going to make the first move; it was Bromley's business. 'Lavinia,' he said, thumping one shaggy creature on the back. 'Two breed certificates.' He nodded at me proudly. 'Championship material.'

'What are you feeding them?' I asked.

'Oats. Bran. Maize. Mix it myself, on scientific principles.'

'I thought they ate anything.'

'Oh yes, they do,' he said vaguely. 'They do.' We were at opposite ends of the goathouse. The animals were all staring at him now, following him round with their eyes. 'There's no need to be afraid of them,' he said. 'They won't bite.'

I patted one cautiously. It didn't even turn its head. 'Why are they all inside?' I said.

'It's only for the midday feed. To stoke them up. They're going out in a minute.' He walked back towards me with the empty scoop. The pairs of eyes, malign, their oblong pupils dilated in the dark, swung round in his wake. 'There's one out there now, you may have seen,' he said. 'Zena. Ca-constipated. That's her problem.' He saw me staring at him. 'Needs the grass,' he said. Behind him one of his acolytes belched and began to cud. 'Something the matter?'

'I'm just interested,' I said.

'You're interested, eh? In what?' Oh, he knew. He struck a pose. 'How do I look, then? Not too ropey?'

'No,' I said. 'Much the same.'

He didn't waver. 'I hope so. I'm fit as hell.' We looked at one another. He seemed to be searching. 'Well, Jack,' he looked for confirmation in my eyes, 'what are you up to?'

I braced myself. 'Sorry?'

'What are you doing now, boy?' Irritation had come into his voice. It was all too plausible.

'I run a bookshop.'

'Good, yes. Jolly good,' he said. 'Yes, that's all right,' he said, as though he'd feared worse. He moved off into a little cubicle. I heard water running into a metal pail.

'I got off to a false start, really. I don't suppose it matters though.'

'How d'you mean, a false start?'

'I went into music. I was a musician.'

'Music.' He switched off the tap and returned, listing under the weight of the bucket. 'Music.' He peered at me. 'Did I put you in the Bust-Up revue?'

'Not for that,' I said. 'I usually played Miss Patterson.'

He grunted. 'They were fun, weren't they,' he said without a smile. 'Those sa-silly sketches.' He stood beside me, still holding the bucket.

'They were very good. Especially your performances.' I put a little edge into my voice.

'Really?' He seemed pleased.

'Yes. You were terrific.' He gazed at me soberly again. I felt sure we were on the threshold.

'I'm terribly sorry,' he said. 'I'm so bad at names. What did you say yours was?' It was so heartfelt that I was lost for a moment, and failed to answer. His face creased in acute embarrassment; I felt the ground give way under me. 'Jack something,' he muttered.

'Thurgo.'

'Ah!' he said, apparently none the wiser. 'Ah,' again, and he moved off, spilling the water. He tipped the remains into waiting buckets, a little at a time, moving along the row of stalls. 'I don't remember you as a musician.'

'No,' I said, 'you tried to put me off it.' He stopped to shake his spattered trousers. 'You said music softened the brain.'

'It does,' he said. 'Been proved.'

'That's what you said then. All it did was encourage me.' I could hear a schoolboy tone creeping into my voice.

Bromley was heading back towards me, along the opposite row. 'Well, don't hold me responsible,' he said. 'I warned you.'

'Brain's all right, thank you.'

Something in this seemed to quicken a memory. He stopped; I hoped it was Diophantes. He gazed at me. 'Thurgo,' he said. 'You're a bowler.'

'I was, yes.'

'You're a bowler. That's right, I never knew whether to put you in the team. There was another spinner, wasn't there. Taller than you.'

'Washington.'

'Washington.' Bromley grinned. 'He was pretty good for his age. Did you ever get into the team?'

'Yes,' I protested. 'My last year.'

A sly grin came over his face. 'I thought I kicked you out for fooling around in the nets.' I grinned back. It was the old Bromley. 'Yes, I did. Didn't I. Thurgo. You were a lazy sod. What are you doing now?'

'I'm running a bookshop.'

'You told me that,' he said serenely. 'I mean *now*. Are you on holiday, or what?' I nodded. 'On your own? Do you want to stay?

We'll put you up, these stalls are pretty comfortable.' The school-masterly tone lingered into the invitation, a little incongruously. I felt a surge of sympathy for the man trapped in the bantering relationship with sniggering pupils, now faced with the grown-up product. Our manner had nowhere to go but back; and I could sense his own distaste at it. 'Stay as long as you like,' he said, trying to bed in a new chumminess. 'Only joking about the stalls, there's plenty of room indoors.'

'That's very kind of you.'

'Well, I've got to make it up to you, haven't I?'

'How d'you mean?'

The slyness crept back. 'Your false start,' he said lightly. The mouth was set, the eyes danced, and all my suspicions came back in a rush.

'Not at all,' I mumbled.

'Really—we'd be delighted. Come and go as you please. As long as you're up at five to do the milking.' His smile wavered. 'Will you stay?' The hint of pleading undid me again, and I felt ashamed of my motives for coming. It must have showed. 'Well, you'll stay for lunch. And tea, perhaps.'

'Of course.' I couldn't carry on with this. 'John…' I said.

'Yes?'

'There's a reason I came. That is, other than—'

'—old times' sake. Yes.' He paused. 'Look, that's all right.' But I needed a moment to settle into our new roles; he studied me. 'You want me to sort something out. A problem.'

He gave a knowing smile, and it tugged me adrift. 'You mean you know what I'm talking about?'

'Not the first idea,' he said cheerfully. 'Something on your mind, is there? Well, don't be shy.'

I held his gaze; for the first time he looked at ease. 'I thought you were in an accident. In Norfolk.'

Bromley seemed more confused than taken aback. 'You thought

I was in an accident?'

'Yes.'

He paused. 'I'm sorry. I don't understand. You *thought* I was?'
I nodded. 'D'you mean a dream?'

'No. Definitely not a dream. There was a car crash. I was the
first to reach the accident, the driver was dead but his passenger
was thrown clear. They put him in a cottage hospital, in Cley.' I
watched his face. *Cly*, I'd pronounced it. 'Or *Clay*,' I said.
Bromley looked blankly back, waiting. 'He's on his way to Norwich
now, unless he's come round. When I last saw him he was in a
coma.'

'In a coma? Poor chap.' He seemed to be suppressing a smile.
'Go on.'

'That's all. I thought he was you.'

'Good Lord.'

'I was sure he was.'

Bromley stood nodding at me, affable. 'Really? Then what? Did
you... ta-tell the police?' I searched his eyes for a clue, but he was
all innocence. Behind us a goat banged her pail angrily, demanding
more, while Bromley waited for my reply.

'Yes.'

He set off towards the bolshy goat. 'Did you. What did they say?'

'Well, there was a woman who identified him. As someone called
Arthur Sindacombe.'

'Arthur Sindacombe.' Bromley removed the bucket and returned.
Now he was smiling openly. 'You say a woman identified him.'

'Yes.' It seemed an odd remark of his. 'He looked like you. I
didn't know what to think.'

'Ah. I get you,' he grinned. '*I* see.'

Behind us the goathouse door opened, flooding Bromley with light.
He looked grey, almost made-up, in the piercing sunshine. I looked
round. 'Come along, Johnny,' said Mrs Bromley, in a tone I'd never
heard used to his face.

94

He kept his eyes on me. 'Yes, I get you,' he repeated. 'You mean, you thought it was me having ... a little escapade ...'

I was conscious of Laura Bromley at my back, and quickly shook my head. Bromley was not to be deterred. 'So you came down here to—what? Sniff around? Is that it?' His delight grew, filling the smoky hut. 'And I thought you'd come to consult the oracle! D'you hear that?'—now addressing his wife—'This chap ... this is Thurgo,' he explained; she nodded patiently. 'I remember him. The little sneak: thought I was on the razzle there in Norfolk. With some woman.' There was a silence behind me. 'Thought he'd caught me with a totty!' Bromley's grin was huge, the yellow teeth withdrawn. I looked round.

Mrs Bromley frowned in disbelief. 'Who—*Johnny?*'

'What do you mean?' came his voice. 'D'you think I'm past it?'

'Bring him, will you,' she said to me. 'Lunch is waiting.'

'Let it wait! I'm interrogating a sneak!'

But Mrs Bromley was gone, leaving the door open behind her.

'And shut the door!' he added. We waited for a moment, in vain.

The reflex surged up in me. 'Were you born in a cave?' I said it softly, but Bromley picked it up at once.

'What?'

I grinned. He looked back at the door, pleased at my prompting.

'Yes.' He swelled up, and bellowed it. 'Shut the door! Were you ba-born in a cave?!' Then, seeing my expression, 'Don't *you* laugh. I should have kicked you out. Fooling around at fielding practice—I should have packed you off for good!' He gleamed at me; I was only too happy to play along, pupil again. Bromley saw it in my eyes, and drew back to switch on the P.O.W. camp Kommandant for me. I saw his mouth prepare for the Teutonic hiss. 'So! We have found the troublemaker!'

I shook my head, and made to answer.

'You continue to deny it? Hans!' He turned to the nearest goat, which was watching avidly; then, lowering his voice: 'Bring ... the 'milking stool' . . . as we call it here at Stalag Seventeen.' The hut inmates continued cudding; Bromley gestured largely at them. 'You see these men? Under my command they have become... *animals!*' A giggle began to form in his voice. 'They know their places! Soon you too will be . . . milking . . . obediently!'

His face became a rictus, fighting back the grin. But the expression I saw breaking through was one of disgust with himself. I watched, helpless. His features slowly calmed, averted, surveying the animals, until the dignity of the goat judge assumed its place. The old voice returned.

'Come on, sneak, let's have some grub. We'll let the goats out afterwards.'

He strode quickly out of the hut.

IN THE AFTERNOON Bromley and I led the goats to the upper slopes. Rather, we followed them, as they mooched from bramble patch to bramble patch, keeping ahead of us, nipped ends of blackberry shoots in their soft mouths. Bromley wore a Basque beret. He looked much more becalmed than he had at school. After a winning match, especially on a rival school's ground, there was always a fierce satisfaction in his eye; he'd lean across the driver and hold the car horn blaring all the way up the school drive. This was a new, serene Bromley by my side. But it brought back Bromley moods I'd forgotten, Bromley listening to classical music in his room, gesturing silently at us to return the borrowed books to their shelves and be gone; Sunday Bromley, glimpsed on a solitary walk in the bracken, along the railway line. It also brought back with an odd clarity as though I were seeing Bromley in a dream—as though I could stretch out my hand and touch his unshaven cheek but he wouldn't feel it because I was visiting him from another dimension—the precise feelings he used to evoke in me, which I'd only thought I remembered up till now, till it was *him*, unquestionably him, him with his histrionic and expressive capacities, as David's book put it, restored: Bromley troubled, real, not the totem pole in the hospital bed. Yes, I *had* loved him. And it was like wanting him as a father, but not as *my* father. Yes, that was it, I'd wanted him as another father, not one to replace the tall besuited man in Mother's photographs, the man with the big nose who looked tamed and subdued by his baggy 'Forties suit, but a different father, one who was a rough bear I alone could tease and chide and tame. I quite enjoyed the fact that Father was dead, or at least accepted without distress that I had photographs for a father, and it was so hard to get my mother's full attention that the idea of a second parent held no charms—it never occurred to me to picture someone else at home in our cramped flat, much less—absurd idea!—picture Bromley himself at table with Mother and me. Yet looking at him now I was sure I *would* have made a father of him whether my own had been alive or not; it was simply an affection he inspired in me, a desire, I realized now with surprise, to comfort, even to father him; this was good—surely I was here for this, to say farewell to my childhood and to recognize that the Bromley beside me, this walking talking Bromley, was no more than a retired schoolmaster putting on a show for an old pupil. Or trying not to, perhaps, I wasn't sure. He knew I was watching him.

'I think I've made out pretty well. Don't you? All this,' we surveyed his new house, and the fields, 'and Laura—stroke of luck at my age.'

Lunch had been rather silent. At intervals Laura and Bromley had enquired about my life since leaving school; and Bromley wanted to hear about my school contemporaries. The Trevelyan story, Trev as sleuth-cum-criminal, was a great success. He made me repeat it, over coffee, and told me in return some of Trev's grimier exploits at The Arbor. There was hardly a word between husband and wife. She seemed anxious to get us out again, and swept off Bromley's unfinished coffee into the kitchen. 'But I like it cold,' protested Bromley. 'Rubbish,' came the reply. Bromley smiled knowingly at me, as though proud of these attentions and, glancing at the kitchen where Laura was emptying the cup, leant towards me. 'Mad as a teapot,' he murmured. I grinned; this was a Bromley phrase whose origin was handed down in school lore. Before my time, an annual cricket match had been held against a local hospital, by repute a lunatic asylum. On one occasion, one of their bowlers had stopped dead at the end of his run, just as he was about to deliver the ball. With one arm pointing forwards and the other back, he stood there for a while on one leg, statuesque, then whispered to the umpire, 'I'm a teapot: pour me out.' Bromley was the umpire, and he handled it impeccably. He stepped forward, unsmiling, bent the bowler to the horizontal like a tango partner, and poured him out. The man thanked him politely and finished the over. Mad as a teapot became Bromley's favourite reproof.

The goats were spreading out across the mountainside, in little groups. 'I met her on a cruise,' said Bromley.

'A cruise?'

'To Greece. Didn't you see the slides?' I searched my memory; no slides. 'After your time, perhaps,' he said, and sat down heavily. 'I got the bells there.' He nodded at the goats, now tinkling faintly in the distance. 'And the idea,' he said fondly: house and herd were laid out beneath us. 'Wedding bells and all.'

'And what about Diophantes?' I said. He stared, but I knew the penny would drop; the Diophantes question had been a Bromley standby. 'You told us he was wrong.' Bromley slid his jaw sideways, reflectively. He'd forgotten my triumph.

'The answer's eighty-four,' he said. 'Is that the one?'

Well, he was entitled to forget; $\frac{7}{7} bachelor = right$ was a thing of the past. Bromley had turned back to the view, and we sat in silence, gazing at the village and the fields. I felt restless; at the same time I was happy just sitting there with him. Eventually he tucked up his legs and settled, straightbacked, watching his goats as if he'd studied the role in Greece. I lay back in the grass. A buzzard swayed in the warm air, above us; bees hummed in my ear.

'You're not married, then,' said Bromley.

'No.'

'No. You do good deeds.'

I'd told him about our plans to house Hammersmith's community centre on Sue's premises. He hadn't wanted to hear much about the shop; he'd never been interested in books, or in America. 'I haven't started yet,' I said. In fact I had stood in now and again at the citizen's advice bureau, giving uninformed advice, and I'd exaggerated this to Bromley, hoping to capture his interest. 'At least, not getting paid for it.'

'I should hope not,' he said. 'Oi,' he called to a goat who was biting another's hindquarters. They were too far away to hear. 'Rather you than me,' he went on. 'Or don't you mind it? Listening to other people's problems.'

'No. I don't mind.'

'I do.'

'I don't mind listening,' I said. 'It's giving them advice, that's the difficult part.'

'I'll do that bit,' said Bromley solemnly. 'You listen to them for a couple of hours, then I'll walk in and tell them what to do.'

'All right.'

'Catch the first train out, that's what I'd tell them. Get a good woman and get the hell out.'

'I'll pass it on.'

'Will you?' said Bromley, suddenly amused. He turned to me, back to where I lay with my head in the grass. 'No you won't, Thurgo. Will you. They don't want to stir their stumps, your citizens.' He turned back to the goats and snorted, shaking his head. 'The buggers haven't got the legs.'

I fidgeted for a while, in silence. 'What about you?' Bromley said without looking round. I sat up and picked some grass, shredding it. 'Got a good woman?'

I nodded.

'Nothing to stop you then, is there?'

I eyed the goats; they were at peace again. Bromley followed my gaze. 'Get off the pot, Thurgo.' I picked more grass. 'Your wretched citizens. It's them or you, boy.' He paused. 'Them or you. And they're going to survive, you know that, don't you. They're dug in there, in their armchairs.' He glanced at me; I smiled at my grass. 'Got their orders for the day.' The Kommandant returned, softly this time, a monotone. 'Salute the Führer, take your pills, switch on the news, for you the war is over.' I said nothing. He resumed, without the accent. 'Everyone's gone home.'

Bromley was studying me.

'You've grasped that, have you?' he said.

'Sir,' I nodded, idly. Gone home? No-one I knew had gone home, or was going home. David perhaps, home in Chicago; or was he coming home to Cley? Bromley was still intent.

'There's no-one there,' he said.

I smiled. 'Except the Kommandant.'

'No! Dolt!' Bromley glared at me, then subsided. 'Dolt. They don't need a Kommandant any more.' I nodded, to placate him. 'He's dead. *Kaputt.*' Bromley smiled down at my puzzled face. 'I hardly do him any more,' he said lightly. Below us a goat bell clanged. I saw the slyness in Bromley's face. 'Even I know when to stop the foolery,' he said, 'Thurgo.'

Now I was utterly at sea; I had supposed he was talking about city life; now he was talking about his school charades. Or more than school charades? 'How was Aberdeen?' I said.

'Aberdeen? My God,' he lowered his eyebrows at me. 'You sneak. No, it was splendid, simply splendid. Talked goats.' He eyed me, and returned my teasing tone. 'Splendid animals, in Aberdeen.'

I held his look. 'And what precisely makes a good goat?' I said, but he ignored it and turned back to the herd.

'That must have been a ghost you saw. Your Norfolk laddie,' he said after a time. 'Or a psychic foretaste of the future: I'm going there next week, to judge. At Diss.'

'In a boater?'

'A boater? Why, did I appear to you in a boater?'

I stared him out. 'It wasn't a ghost, John.'

'Of course it was,' said Bromley. 'We're all ghosts now.' He gazed out keenly at the view, the valley and the hills beyond, as though to spy something. The prospect was magnificent; I looked with him in silence. I imagined my mother, striding across the bare places to rendezvous with demons. Bromley looked down at the houses in the spinneys by the river, snug as nesting birds. I felt a sudden yearning for their cover.

'There's nothing there,' Bromley said quietly. 'For the flesh.' I glanced at him. 'Nothing left,' he said. 'It doesn't mean a thing any more. This whole valley: it goes right through us. Out the other side.' He swivelled to me as if to offer his transparency, smiling. 'Don't you see that?'

'No.'

He laughed affectionately and watched me as I shredded grass. 'Come. Be a happy ghost,' he said.

'I am,' I protested under my breath.

'Good. I'm a very happy ghost,' said Bromley. 'Tending my flock.'

TEA WAS GRIM. Laura sat sphinx-like, hands curled forwards on the fluted arm-rests of her chair. The food, stiff and perfectly distributed on the white tablecloth, looked like painted plaster moulds. Bromley had changed into appropriate clothes. I felt unclean.

'You're in no rush, are you?' Laura boomed as I bolted my fiery tea. 'You're welcome to stay. If there's no train.' Bromley stared at his cup and appeared not to hear.

'No, there's a train all right,' I said. 'I've checked.'

She nodded in undisguised relief. Perhaps it was my clothes that made me unwelcome; or was it my suspicions, as Bromley had revealed them in the goathouse? And my possible collusion with her husband? I couldn't tell from her face; her features were unresponsive, as though they had been tauter once but had grown baggy with use; big features, notably a large, wide, oddly unyielding mouth, friendly when it smiled. In repose it was as if its width had only served to taste more disappointment.

Bromley squinted at his cup. 'No milk?' he said mournfully.

Laura continued to stare at me. 'There's no milk, I'm afraid,' she said to me, as though it were some kind of blessing.

'What have you done with it?' asked Bromley.

'It's what *you've* done with it, dear.' She smiled at me. 'He gives it to the kids.' And turning to him, 'You didn't save any, did you.'

'Didn't I?'

Laura poured herself another cup. 'Scones,' she said, and passed a plate.

Bromley stood. 'I'll go and milk one quickly, shall I?'

'Not in those clothes, Johnny.'

'Oh. Right.' He stood there, poised. I took a scone. 'Did you want some milk?' he asked, turning to me. I shook my head.

'He's just being polite. Aren't you, Jack,' smiled Mrs Bromley.

'No. I don't take milk.'

'Sit down, Johnny.' Laura passed me the plain cake. 'Twenty goats outside the door,' she said, 'and no milk.'

'Well, our babies need their daily pinta, don't they?' Bromley said, settling in again.

'Your babies, dear,' said Laura lightly. 'Nothing to do with me.'

Bromley grinned at me for support. 'Come. Where are your maternal instincts?'

'You know where they are, dear,' she said, in the same tone as before.

'Do I?' said Bromley.

Laura turned to me. 'Do you live in Norfolk now?'

I could feel Bromley swelling up. 'What do you mean?' he insisted.

'Where *do* you live?' smiled Laura. I opened my mouth to reply.

'You sacrificed them for the greater good,' said Bromley. She turned and eyed him tenderly.

'Don't be an ass,' she said. I watched the Kommandant take shape on Bromley's lips. Then he thought better of it. Laura turned back to me. 'When did you say your train was?'

'I don't know,' I said. 'It goes from Builth Road.'

There was a pause. 'Filth Road,' said Bromley, and chuckled quietly into his tea. There was a silence. I gazed at my empty cup.

'We can ring up and find out,' Laura said. 'Johnny can do that.'

'At once,' said Bromley, sobering.

'Don't worry,' she confided to me. 'I'll drive you.'

I glanced at Bromley. 'I don't drive,' he said, drawing himself up. 'I reject the machine, and it rejects me. It's a mutual antipathy. I failed the test.'

'Four times,' said Mrs Bromley.

Bromley evaded my eyes. 'Just making sure,' he said.

The goats were strolling down the hill, bells clanking, in procession, to the goathouse. A fine mane of hair glowed on their backs, in the early evening light. Bromley and I stood by the garage, watching them, as Laura brought the car out. Around the animals, the bare slope was transformed by shadows, every tussock, every bramble featured by the level sun. The goats ignored them now, ambling back for better things.

'Look at them,' Bromley sighed, 'the buggers.' I watched the mountain, its bare dome crowned in a last cone of light.

The car, a gleaming Rover, drew up and I got in beside Laura. Bromley tapped softly on the window. I wound it down.

He bent towards me, ignoring his wife. 'We're all ghosts now, Thurgo,' he said firmly. 'Ra-remember that.' I nodded. He tapped sharply on the car roof, twice, and straightened up out of sight. Mrs

Bromley put the car in gear, noisily. 'Time to go home,' said Bromley. We rattled off down the narrow track.

The goats filtering down the hill, rubbing sides, the cloud of their several breath golden in the light; the sound of bells. In Birmingham I walked blindly back to the same hotel. The woman offered me a different room, identical.

'This one all right, love?'

I nodded.

Empty sky. Buzzards; Mother meeting Bromley on the cold hillside. Nothing there, for the flesh. Splendid animals. Ghosts now, snug as nesting birds. Ra-remember that. Time to go home.

In the morning I ordered kippers.

'THERE WAS A message from the cottage hospital. Mrs Stevenson rang.'

'Oh?'

'Sindacombe wants to see you. He's come round, it seems they didn't have to pack him off to Norwich after all.'

'Wants to see *me?*' I said.

Sue had brought Stefanie along to Sheringham station, and now the child was looking round at me from the front seat of the Triumph, with an unsettling smile. I smiled back, but her expression didn't waver. Something was up. It was sweltering, thundery at last. Even a windy ride in the open car couldn't dispel the atmosphere.

'He wants to thank you.'

'Me? Why?'

'Who knows,' said Sue. 'For holding his hand, I suppose.' She smiled to herself. I had told her Bromley was there, in Wales, after all; as Sue had forecast. But I felt able to ignore her smiles. The Sindacombe business had been a signal, I was sure, telling me to find Bromley and go to the mountain. Perhaps it wasn't what the Master would have called a short cut, but he wouldn't have called it a mistake either. There was no such thing as a mistake.

'Sindacombe's all right, is he?' I asked, glancing at Stefanie as well. The child made no response.

'We haven't checked.' Sue glanced at me. 'We could drop by now, if you like. Unless you want to get straight back. Have you eaten? I'm afraid we have.'

I nodded. 'On the train.' Winding its way through Leicestershire and Lincolnshire, the fields ripe, the banks of dark foliage poised between blossom and berry, waiting for the rain. I tried to think of Sindacombe in his hospital bed.

'Tell him,' grinned Stefanie. 'About Claire.'

'Don't be silly, Stef,' said Sue mildly.

'What about Claire?'

'Nothing.'

'Tell him,' the child insisted.

'Shut up, you,' said Sue. She glanced at me again. 'I'm singing tonight, in Colchester. You're welcome to come along. Or you can stay, it's up to you.'

'I'll come along.'

'Claire's boyfriend's been,' sang Stefanie, and bounced with glee as if uncorked at last.

'Sit properly!'

Stefanie had turned round to me again, swivelling on her seat so that her back was to the windshield and her legs tucked under her. The wind parted her hair, and blew it so hard it almost met again in front of her face. 'She's going to a party. On her own.'

'Not unless *you're* prepared to go to Diana's for the night,' Sue said, 'or Jack decides to stay home and look after you.'

'What is all this?' I said.

'Steffie says Claire's been having boyfriend trouble.' Sue was grinning at the road ahead. 'She hasn't said a word to me.'

'It's tonight, the party!'

'Do turn round,' I told the child sternly, 'at this speed.' She gazed back, smirking like Sue, and I turned to the window to avoid them both.   Shadowless, the neat fields stretched away, the barley still before the thunder. It was the wind, the bald hills that drew me, not this tidy, profitable grid, this horizontal office block.   Get a good woman and get the hell out. Well, Bromley was convincing on the hillside; less convincing in the home. But I didn't have to end up like him. Besides, I was no goatherd. I began to work on the idea of a country bookshop. Nothing folksy. Erudition in the mountains.

'Tell me about Bromley,' Sue said.

'He hasn't changed a bit. Madder, if anything. He was all right with me.' I didn't really want to share it. 'The marriage is a disaster.'

Sue said nothing. I forebore to ask about David, at that moment. I suspected there was no news; she'd have mentioned it.

'I must tell you,' I said. 'I wrote a poem this morning, in the hotel.' I paused and grinned. 'You might find it appropriate.'

'Oh yes?'

'It starts ... *The day that I became a monk*,' I saw Sue smile; '*I got into a holy funk.*' They both laughed. I joined in.

'Yes...' went Sue.

I hesitated.   Another time. 'It's rather rude, the next bit,' I explained. 'And I don't think I can remember all of it. Not in front of children, anyway.' I passed my hand over Steffie's face, to shush her objections. 'What's more I've gone and lost it. It was in the book, the Sufi book, I wrote it in the back. I must have left it somewhere—in the train, I think. Or in the waiting room.'

'Oh Jack,' said Sue, sounding like my mother.

It was true; I'd hunted for it. 'I went back and looked,' I said.

Sue smiled. 'It was not in fact there,' she said in Sufi style. 'Lose your head next.'

We drew up at the cottage hospital, setting a new speed record for the driveway. I got out gratefully and made my way alone, into the office. Mrs Stevenson didn't seem at all pleased to see me.

'What is it now?' she said, from a cluttered desk.

'I've come to see Arthur Sindacombe. At his request.'

She frowned impatiently. 'You're much too late. He went yesterday morning.'

'Oh,' I said. 'Well, that's good news.' She looked at me for a moment, then down at her papers.

Yesterday morning: I suddenly began to register. I was off my guard.

'I wouldn't call it good,' she said. 'We didn't think he was ready.'

'*When?*' I said.

'Yesterday.' She looked up.

'When? Early?'

She nodded, trying to gauge my stare.

My mind was racing. 'How?' I demanded. 'How *could* he go?'

She shook her head. 'He was up. We couldn't force him to stay, once he was out of shock.'

I glanced at the window. Sue and Stefanie were only yards away, inside the car, motionless.

'His wife collected him,' came Mrs Stevenson's voice.

Time enough. Full speed, back to Builth Wells. Filth Wells. Laughing into his teacup: poor old Thurgo, always a step behind. 'By car?'

'Well, she didn't make him *walk* home. What *is* this about?'

'Did you ever meet Mrs Langley?' I asked. 'The lady who—the landlady—'

'Yes. She came on Monday.'

I felt anger rising. 'Is *she* Mrs Sindacombe?'

'What?'

'Is she the same woman?'

Mrs Stevenson smiled at me, exasperated. 'I don't understand.'

'They couldn't be the same person?'

She pushed her chair back. 'Mr Thurgo...'

'Would you mind describing Mrs Sindacombe?' She stood up in

silence, giving me a humouring look. 'Please,' I said. 'Please.'

'I can't help you very much. Matron was in charge. As far as I can remember, Mrs Sindacombe was just a girl.'

'A girl?' A girl. I shook my head and took a step towards the full-length window. Sue was gazing at me from the car. She looked a little disconcerted. I was grinning all over my face.

IT WAS IN in fact so, then, after all—so much for Sufi wisdom! I lay in the deckchair in Sue's back garden, waiting for the storm, and chortled. The girls watched my performance, warily. There was something in me I couldn't place, seeking an outlet. They knew it too. The weather had brought Steffie's tortoise out from under his bush. He stretched his head from side to side like a mechanical toy. He too eyed me as if I were cracking up.

'Find a good woman . . . the old hypocrite!' I took it out on the tortoise. Nothing left for the flesh, eh? Nothing left in Builth Wells, obviously. A happy ghost, tending his flock. I'd lapped it up.

'All right,' said Sue. 'Suppose it's Bromley—'

'Suppose? You're joking. He had ample time, by car.'

'Just let me make my point,' she warned. I waited. She seemed to think better of it.

'Say it.'

Sue shook her head once, briefly. I watched her. It was chokingly still, in the garden.

'You don't just come out of a coma and walk off,' said Claire. Her tone was gentler; there was an invitation in it I no longer felt like fighting, despite Steffie's prurient looks at both of us in turn. I smiled.

'Well, it seems he did. This . . . girl just turned up, and he came right round.' I looked at Sue. 'She insisted on taking him away.'

'I don't see what's so goddamn suspicious. She wanted to look after him herself.' Sue saw my expression. 'Jack, she's his wife.'

108

'I hope not. Because then it's bigamy.' The tortoise neck had stopped waving; now it poked out further from its shell, as if testing for rain. I turned to Claire. 'You believe me, don't you?' But she hesitated.

Sue chuckled. 'She thinks you're mad.'

'In that case,' I said, 'I'm not coming to your party.' Even Steffie had the tact to look down. Claire glanced at Sue and saw her grin into her lap. She smiled, relaxing. 'I don't think you're mad.'

'Right,' I crowed. 'There you are.'

'Oh Jack,' said Sue, 'it's nonsense, utter nonsense. What about the landlady? If *she's* not Bromley's mistress—'

'Totty,' I put in. 'He might have dozens.'

'Just suppose she isn't.'

'All right,' I said. I'd been working on this one. 'Suppose she isn't. Doesn't make the slightest difference.'

'Yes it does. She knows the Sindacombes.'

'Ah,' I said. 'That's where you're wrong. I talked to her that day. I know the story.' I rose out of the deckchair and walked a few paces, forcing their attention. Only the tortoise failed to turn.

'Go on.'

'Well,' I began. 'Let's assume Mrs Langley's telling the truth—all right? According to her, it was Mrs Sindacombe who used to come to Cromer, with her ailing mother, to stay at the boarding house. No Mr Sindacombe. He hated the seaside, that's what Mrs Langley gathered. Next thing, the mother dies. Buried at Cromer—she'd been living there at Mrs Langley's, at the end.' I paused. 'Obviously hated *Mr* Sindacombe, that's my theory. Anyway, Mrs Sindacombe still comes to Cromer, to put flowers on the grave. Alone. One day, while she's staying at Mrs Langley's—*while* she's staying there—up she turns with a natty-looking gent, saying, look: my husband's suddenly arrived. This was four years ago, just after a certain schoolmaster retired. Since then "Mr Sindacombe" has become mysteriously reconciled to the seaside. They come every summer,' I smiled round at the ladies, 'to put flowers on Mother's grave.'

'It won't do, Jack,' Sue laughed. 'What about the Mr Sindacombe who used to hate the seaside? Why would Mrs Sindacombe have bothered to invent *him?*'

'She didn't. He's real. Don't you see? One day Bromley comes to Cromer, to see a man about a goat, say. Meets Mrs Sindacombe, tickles her fancy, she says: come back to the boarding house, I can introduce you as my husband—it's all right, the landlady's never met him...'

'Come *on.* Why would she take the risk?'

'Because old Sindacombe, the real one, really hates the seaside. The coast is clear—as far as *he's* concerned, Cromer's become a shrine to his mother-in-law. There's no risk.'

'Bunk,' said Sue.

I was getting nettled. 'You just don't want to believe it.'

'Why *should* I believe it?'

'Why fight it?' I let an edge creep into my voice. I didn't care. 'That's the *point.*'

'You mean . . . you think I don't want to believe that husbands have affairs?' she mocked. 'Don't be a child.'

Steffie broke the silence, unaffected. '*I* think it's the landlady,' she announced with finality. I didn't know what she meant, but I was grateful all the same.

'Oh?'

'She's lying,' offered the child.

'Well, she could be, yes. She could be inventing the whole thing. But who's the girl, then, the one who collected him from hospital? Who's Mrs Sindacombe?' It dawned on me then with hideous simplicity—the idea took flesh in seconds—the accident, just down the road from here, so close, perhaps on his way here . . . I stared at the others in turn. 'My God: it's not either of *you,* is it?'

For a moment they didn't speak; but from their faces I knew I was losing my grip. 'One of us?' Sue gasped, and the tension dissolved in helpless giggles.

'Well, never mind,' I muttered. Steffie rolled around as though it was the best joke yet. I looked away, up at the threatening clouds, and back at my unprotected bicycle. A plan presented itself: settle it.

'I'm going to Cromer.'

'Now?' The laughter only rose.

'Get hold of the landlady,' I said, raising my voice. Sue had sobered, but I ignored her pitying glance, and turned to Claire. 'I'll get back in time,' I said. She nodded, awkward. 'When's it start, the party?'

'I'll wait,' she said, unduly casual, but not casual enough to stem Steffie's further giggles. We ignored her.

I could still feel Sue's gaze. 'Don't you see,' I said, still locked in, 'if I get Mrs Langley talking about Sindacombe and what he's like, she's bound to give the game away.' Sue nodded; it was her first concession, and I felt ashamed of my earlier tone. '*If* he's Bromley,' I said as a peace offering.

'Why don't you just leave it, Jack,' she said gently. 'God knows, it doesn't matter now.'

'No, you're right,' I said. 'It doesn't. I'm just curious.'

'Like hell,' she said, low.

I waited. 'What do you mean?' But she didn't answer. In my vanity I took it, at the time, for jealousy, the way she had of treating me as her property. 'I just want to know if I've been had,' I said.

Sue gave a private, husky laugh. Behind us the first thunder rolled at last from the horizon, as if answering my last remark.

'D-Damn . . . right!' I echoed in Bromley tones.

MRS LANGLEY'S BACK room was as full of furniture, knick-knacks, and paintings, as the entrance hall and reception room through which

I'd passed were bare. The difference was so striking that at first I thought the hotel was being redecorated, its breakables stored for safety's sake in the owner's quarters. But Mrs Langley moved through the clutter with practised agility and I saw on closer inspection that these were all mementoes, and belonged. High up on one crowded dresser a television set broadcast listlessly, the sound faint and muzzy, as if dying slowly of neglect. Flashes of static lashed the picture in time with the lightning: outside, the storm had begun. Mrs Langley took an armchair by the window, hands clenched, tears wetting her face as she talked of Arthur Sindacombe. I tried to tell myself that she was an emotional woman, that I hadn't simply put my foot in it again. The accent, as near as I could place it, was central European. Chrissie's aunts cried easily.

The rain had held off as I cycled before the wind, along the coast to Cromer. Fifty minutes of sheer pleasure, with few hills and a following gale sweeping me down the road. A girl; a party, to return to. Grey breakers to my left, thundering up the beaches. I saluted the grassy turrets of the horror-film hotel as I raced through empty Sheringham. West Runton, East Runton, flecks of sea spray in my face; I was the herald of the storm, and beat it by minutes into Cromer.

Behind the tear-stained face the windowpanes showed rain sweeping vengefully across the pier.

'They had a row,' sighed Mrs Langley. 'Oh, it was such a silly thing! The hat...'

'The straw hat?'

'He lost it, in a pub. He left it there.'

'A straw boater? With a blue band?'

She turned and looked past the lace curtains, abstracted. She wore no make-up, and her face looked weary, ugly with a long restraint of anger. I could imagine it, set for defeat, over a Bingo card in one of the innumerable neon-lit halls lining the gloomy streets as I rode in. Cromer appeared to be the Bingo capital of the world.

In the hallway of the hotel she had embraced me like a fellow-mourner and drawn me by the hand into her room, as though I had come quite naturally, out of sympathy, to share her grief.

'He didn't like the hat,' said Mrs Langley firmly. '*She* bought it for him. She said it made him look younger.'

'And he lost it, did you say?' Mrs Langley nodded; this was apparently no more than 'she', the wife, deserved. 'But he had a straw hat with him, didn't he? It was found in the van, after the accident.'

'Oh yes, it came back,' she said without looking at me. 'They always do.' She paused. I saw a string of obedient boaters trailing Bromley down the promenade like a grounded kite. 'He's always losing things,' she went on, 'and they always come back. He says he could leave his wallet in the street and it would come back.'

'That sounds like him,' I said. 'How did the boater come back?'

'Some people from the pub, they brought it back. She was annoyed: they made fun of the hat. She said they were rude, she didn't like their language, and she asked Arthur not to see them again. And he refused. And then you should have heard *her* language, silly bitch.'

'Who were the people?' I asked.

'Just friends, friends of Arthur's,' she said. 'He has so many friends here. And he told me she was jealous, but I think she was angry about the hat, that was the reason. The stupid hat.' She sighed. 'She's very young. And then she took the car and drove away, and . . . he was so upset—' She faltered, fighting back more tears. Her head turned and her gaze crossed me, coming to rest on the back wall. 'I'm sorry,' she said, brimming. New memories were flooding in. 'Oh poor man.'

She was longing to tell someone; a friend of Arthur's. I had said I'd worked with him, on a farm, with goats. The word evinced no surprise, I noted; but no recognition either. And all I'd heard since I arrived were tales of the Sindacombe ménage, on holiday. Mrs

Langley was still looking away, waiting to be prompted. 'What happened?' I said.

There came a knock on the door, timid but insistent. Mrs Langley released the embroidered covers on the arm of her chair, which she was clutching, and smoothed them absently.

'I mustn't tell you.'

'Someone's at the door.'

'Go away!' The anger rose up, transferred itself to me. 'What do you *think* happened?'

I nodded, lost. The knocking came again.

'I didn't mean to make it worse,' she said, wiping her face.

'I understand.'

'He was here, he sat here. Sunday night. He said he'd stay here, come and live here, the bloody fool, I knew he wouldn't. We were both a little tiddly.' She glanced at me, and away again. 'And we went upstairs. You're old enough to understand.' I nodded; she made a snuffly noise, a laugh. 'He didn't do it, he was too drunk. Poor dear man, he thought he had. I didn't like to tell him in the morning.' Her laughter spluttered. 'Excuse me. And he went out and . . .' she gestured dramatically, 'didn't come back. They say he was drinking, somewhere. With this man, the plumber.' I nodded at her glance, solicitous. 'You see? If it wasn't for me, he would never have been in the accident.'

'It's all right,' I soothed. 'He's all right now.'

The knock returned, loudly this time. The sodden face became abruptly martial. 'Oh go away,' said Mrs Langley curtly. The door opened and a tall girl stood there, fretful, in an ill-fitting uniform.

'It's Mr Hawkins,' she said feebly.

'Not now!' The tears came freely, unhampered. 'Hawkins?' she addressed the wall. 'Who in hell is Hawkins?'

'It's the gentleman in number twelve,' murmured the girl. 'He isn't well.' Mrs Langley snorted, derisive. The girl gave a faint moan. 'I think he's having hysterics.' It came out as hystirics. 'He doesn't like the storm.'

'Doesn't like it?' queried Mrs Langley as though it were her home-made apple sauce.

The girl's voice began to rise. 'He's screaming. Everyone's upset. I don't know what to do. Please, Mrs Langley...'

Mrs Langley giggled. 'Tell him not to be so silly.'

'But he's having hystirics!'

'Oh God almighty.' Mrs Langley rose, gazing at me for sympathy. 'Stay there,' she ordered, muttering as she wrestled her way to the door, and out.

The girl gave me a wan smile, relieved, from the doorway. I smiled back. The television set on the dresser crackled insanely among the photographs and vases, with the thunder. At once a flash of lightning lit the room, and as it faded all the lights went out. A dull groan came from the expiring set.

'Shirley!' came Mrs Langley's voice from somewhere down the corridor. 'Light the candles!'

Shirley went in silence, and I sat in my armchair in the darkened room. Now that the television had stopped crackling, a clock could be heard, ticking sullenly. Dim light from the window lit the wall opposite, where Mrs Langley's mid-European ancestors gazed out from a cluster of frames. A younger man in a stiff RAF tunic smiled out from under a peaked cap; the late Mr Langley perhaps. His widow bellowed faintly in the distance. I knew the tone, from Chrissie's minotaur aunts, who could pass from saccharine to apoplexy in the space of a syllable; I had seen it. Aunt Margot had a musty flat on Fortune Green, lined, like Mrs Langley's room, with portraits. Chrissie and I went there for tea, and once, as Chrissie made to add milk to her aunt's cup, the old lady coyly reminded her that she took no more than a drop of milk: 'I only *frighten* the tea, Christina.' Chrissie giggled—this was a phrase she'd often mimicked for me—and in the process she flooded the cup with enough milk to terrify, by Aunt Margot's standards, a whole urn. Chrissie was laughing too hard to apologize, and only my favoured presence prevented an explosion; but I had seen Aunt Margot's face and it left me more frightened than the tea.

I stood and inspected Mrs Langley's ancestors, by lightning. Frock-coated, some beribboned, they sternly ignored the scene reflected in the glass, the rainsoaked pier and its neglected frivolities. They posed with one foot forwards and their weight on the back foot, leaning modestly on their achievements; any of them could have been Chrissie's grandfather. Mine too, by marriage, if things went according to plan. A stout paternity to shore up the abbreviated Thurgo album. After a time I made my way out of the labyrinth of Mrs Langley's dropleaf tables. The corridor was darker still. Faint candlelight, and groans, came from an open doorway and I walked along until I could just see into it. The window showed bright at the end of the room: candles shone in the windows of the house next door. In front of this, in the room, two shapes loomed on the bed. I could make out the largely bald head of the groaning Hawkins. Beside him, my minotaur was stroking it with infinite gentleness. 'It's only clouds,' she said softly, 'angry, angry clouds.' I went slowly back to the cluttered room.

Shirley was there, distributing nightlights from a tray, making altarpieces of the several dressers. We passed in silence; Hawkins no longer groaned. After a time Mrs Langley returned with a candle and glanced round anxiously, lighting empty armchairs.

'Ah, there you are.' The face was less woebegone, smoother now, after her mission of mercy. The candlelight also helped. 'I didn't mean to cry like that. You see, I haven't talked to anyone. You can't, not in this hole.'

Outside, in the street, something clattered to the ground; the wind was blowing harder than ever. I thought: my bicycle, and hurried over to the window, to peer into the growing darkness. But the noise came from a dustbin lid, now edging its way like a giant crab towards the steps that led down to the pier, back to the sea.

'You're not going, are you?' she said as I bent to retrieve my Peugeot cap.

'I just wanted to hear if there was any news. I'm sure Arthur's all right. Now he's home.' No; that was tactless.

'I haven't heard,' she murmured.

She came and took my hand, composing herself. 'Sit down, just for a little while.' I let myself be led. We took the sofa and she placed the candle without looking, on an adjacent table. 'How did you meet Arthur?' she smiled.

I repeated my story, with embellishments, now adding that I kept goats myself.

'Goats,' she said. 'That's interesting.'

'Yes.' I warmed to the subject. 'It's highly scientific now. How you feed them. We used to talk a lot, about goats.'

'Did you? With Arthur? Yes,' she said, 'he's very interested in people. What they do.'

'Mmh.'

She gave my hand a timid squeeze. 'Did he ever talk about Cromer?'

'Yes,' I said, 'oh yes,' and hurried on. I was here to uncover Bromley, not to invent Sindacombe. 'How did he come to live in Newmarket? I've never asked him.'

'Arthur? He was born there.' She eyed me hopefully. 'You say he talks about Cromer?'

'Yes,' I said. 'He said he liked it. Very much.' She smiled, disappointed; I knew she wanted something more. 'To be honest, I didn't really take it in. He mainly talks about his war.'

'His war?'

'The war. I mean: the last war.'

'He has a medal, doesn't he?'

I gave a grunt. Bromley telling tales again: if he'd got anything for valour we'd never have heard the end of it at school. 'Shellshocked in Italy,' I nodded gravely. 'That's why he stammers.'

She smiled as though she hadn't understood.

'Stutters.'

Still nothing.

'He talks a lot about the camp, doesn't he,' I tried. 'In Germany.'

'He never said.' She looked down. 'He saved a lot of lives right here, you know. He won't have told you.'

'Oh?'

'Two years ago. Part of the cliffs collapsed at East Runton, they have a football field there, very dangerous. And there was a coach, parked. Hanging over the edge. They had to bring them out, the people, one by one, and Arthur was helping, he was helping to calm them, in the bus. He went inside to help, I read it in the paper.'

'Really? In the paper?'

'Oh yes. He never mentioned it himself. But afterwards he let me see the letters he was writing to the council,' her accent was becoming more and more guttural, a maddening counterpart to Bromley's Commandant, a consort, 'about the danger all along the cliffs there. He made them put up a fence. That was also in the papers. He wrote letters to them too.'

'Under . . . his own name?' It was perfunctory; I was getting nowhere.

'Of course under his own name, why not?' She smiled proudly, 'You can mention Arthur Sindacombe in Cromer, people will tell you he was like a tiger. And they put up the fence—he made them do it. I call it Arthur's fence.' The tears welled up. 'Oh yes, he won a medal in the war: *she* told me once. I don't know what it was, what sort of medal.' She looked away. The pier was invisible now, wrapped in a dark mist. 'I'd like to have known what it was,' she said. 'But I'm keeping you now, aren't I.'

'No, of course not,' I said. 'Do you have the time?'

Mrs Langley peered shortsightedly at her watch, over the candle flame. 'You think there is a bus?'

'It's all right, I've got my bicycle.'

'In this weather?' Her hand found my arm. 'You're welcome to stay, we've got room.' The face loomed.

'I don't mind cycling.'

'Would you like a drink?' she said as I stood up again. 'Yes? Good, so would I!' She went and groped in a dresser, pulling out a decanter. 'Talk to me. Don't make me tell you about my life.'

'I can tell you about the medal,' I babbled, 'it was the DSO.'

She turned with a little cry. 'The DSO? That's very good, isn't it?'

'Yes, it's very good, it's the Distinguished Service Order. They did say he'd have got the VC,' I heard myself add, 'but they'd given away too many that year.' I grinned wildly. 'That was his story, anyway.'

'Please,' said Mrs Langley, bringing me my glass. 'Don't make fun of me. He'd never say a thing like that.' She studied me. 'What did he tell you about Cromer? Truthfully.'

'Well. He talked about you.'

'Did he? What did he say?' She felt blindly for the sofa.

'Oh, nice things. I couldn't possibly repeat them.'

She cried silently, cradling her drink. 'He'll come back, won't he.'

'Yes I'm sure he will.'

'It was the first time we were ever alone together.' She gazed at me. 'Please don't go.'

'It's all right.' I came to her. 'I'm here.'

'Tell me about him,' she said, at her drink. I nodded, helpless, as she turned to me. 'Talk about Arthur.'

THE NIGHT WAS well advanced by the time I escaped. It didn't matter. I'd praised Sindacombe, I'd buried Bromley, and I was sick of putting on an act. A party was the last thing I needed. And I couldn't have hurried if I'd wanted to: the tail wind that had sped me into Cromer now admonished every thought of Claire with a gust in my face, making me labour with each thrust of the pedals, going slower and slower. The gale was still blowing in across the Wash, and I found myself tearfully fighting downhill slopes to keep moving forwards at all. Cars hooted as their headlamp beams discovered me weaving across the road, standing up in the saddle. I shouted back at them, and fell in a heap in the wake of an articulated lorry, unbalanced by the sudden absence of the wind. I was unhurt but extremely sorry for myself; I cursed my useless brakes, the pelting rain, the wind, I cursed Mrs Langley and all her ancestors. I swore at Bromley. Out of it came an enormous pleasure. I lay back on the roadside, utterly drenched, listening to the rollers in the darkness, like a beached fish. Car lights played over me and passed on as if I was a local landmark. I revelled in it.

On my back, I gave Bromley voice.

'*The day that I became a monk*
  I got into a holy funk,
  I said, I've got to find a girl
  To fuck or else I'm sunk
  The day that I become a monk!'

This cheered me hugely; this—as conceived in the Birmingham hotel room, half asleep, and completed over the kippers—wasn't erudition in the mountains, but it had gusto. I climbed back on my bicycle again. The frame seemed just a little bent. The wheels revolved erratically but I struggled on in the teeth of the gale.

'*I went up to my local priest,*
  I said, kindly prepare a feast,
  In order that I may indulge myself,
  And know the nature of the beast—
  I thought I'd find that out, at least!
 He said, you'd better try this first,
  And fed me candy till I burst.
  I told him, that's enough for me,
  Baptize me! Let me be immersed!
  Let God and man do what they durst!'

One or two houses, outposts, began to shelter me from the worst of the rain. The lights of Cley beckoned ahead; I waggled forwards, defying the elements, and declaiming.

'*And so I entered holy church,*
Whose holy walls I do besmirch,
And here I rest me till I die.
They beat me with a rod of birch
And heaven's left me in the lurch.'

Newgate Green was ominously dark. But there was a light on in the little flint cottage; an upstairs light. I pushed the bike around the back and hurried to the kitchen door. Once inside, I stood for a moment in the warm darkness, beginning to shiver.

'Claire?' came a small plaintive voice. Steffie; but it didn't come from her bedroom, above.

'It's me,' I said. I went and turned the kitchen lights on. My trail puddled from the door, across the plastic tiles. The voice came again, from beyond the sitting room.

'I've fallen down the stairs.'

I shut my eyes in disbelief; I would have laughed, but all the bumptiousness was draining from me, along with the glee I'd shared with the elements. The house was alien to it, and I stood dripping like an unwelcome ghost from the sea.

'I've hurt myself,' Steffie wailed. I found her on the bottom step and carried her up to her bedroom. She too was feeling sorry for herself, and snuffled softly as I laid her on the bed. I fetched a towel and went to David's study. The house was empty, Claire was evidently gone; my doggerel was prophetic. I changed into my old clothes, from the rucksack, then I went back to examine Steffie's ankle.

There was no swelling, and no complaints came when I gripped and moved it. She looked hopefully at me. 'Does it need a bandage?'

'No.'

'Oh please.'

I towelled my head, and murmured against the towel, 'You're a hypochondriac too.'

'You said I'd sprained it.'

'No. I said you might have.' I removed the towel, testing my hair, and looked at her. Different people needed different things; forsaken widows, lonely children . . . Doctor Thurgo held the answer. 'Are there any bandages?'

'In the bathroom,' she nodded eagerly.

'Where's Claire?' I said.

She gave me a canny look. I waited; but Steffie knew a deal when she saw one. 'Are you going to bandage me or not?'

I headed for the bathroom. As I ransacked the wall cupboards, her voice came, stern.

'You've really made a mess of it,' she called.

'A rotten horrible mess,' I agreed. I found the bandages, and returned to the bedside.

'She sent her boyfriend packing, you know. While you were in Wales.'

I wound the crêpe around her foot. 'Nothing to do with me.'

'Of course it is,' she said, and gazed at me. 'He's called Andy.' I wound the bandage tighter. 'Ow.'

'I'm sorry?'

'That hurt.'

'Oh, that's only the start,' I said. 'Most people need painkillers, for *my* bandaging.'

'I don't want it!' she cried.

'Well you've got it, so shut up.'

'He's forgiven her,' she said vengefully.

'Really?'

'He came back, I heard him downstairs. Tonight.'

I secured the bandage, comfortably now, and looked up at her. 'Well, they ought to be here looking after you. God knows you need

122

it.'

A series of emotions over her child's face. 'Don't tell Mummy they went out,' she said, finally. 'Please. I promised Claire I'd be all right.' For all her guile, I wanted to hug her. She looked pleadingly at me. 'It's my fault. Don't tell Mummy.'

'Why shouldn't I?'

'Because I like Claire. Please.'

Hiding her foot from her, I slipped in the safety pin without touching the flesh beneath the bandage. 'Don't you like me?'

'Yes.' It sounded genuine.

'All done.' I patted her ankle and turned to her, sitting back against the wall. 'You want Claire all to yourself, is that it?'

'No. Why do you say that?' She looked at the counterpane, puzzled, then slipped her legs under the sheets, her feet barely reaching me where I sat and reminding me what it was like to only half fill the great burrow of a bed. 'I don't really understand what's going on.'

'Poor old you,' I smiled. 'I'll tell you what's going on. Nothing. Nobody's doing anything. Nobody's doing anything with anyone, anywhere.' I wasn't trying to patronize her; I meant it. 'Understood?' I said. She nodded, seriously. 'Good,' I said with Bromley firmness. 'That's worth remembering.'

She looked at me, stifling an objection. I got to my feet, 'Now you go to sleep, all right?' and went to the door.

'What happened with the landlady?'

'Nothing. Nothing happened with the landlady.'

Steffie looked disappointed. 'Wasn't she lying?

'No, she wasn't. Nobody's lying.' I switched out the light. 'Except me. I've been lying my head off all night, about Arthur effing Sindacombe, the local hero.' I made to shut the door. 'Goodnight.'

'Don't,' said the child. I left the door ajar. For a moment I could see her face in the light left by the open door and I could see we had the same thought. *Ba-ba-born in a cave?!* I made off before she could ask for the impersonation. 'Is he Sindacombe, then?' came her voice.

'He's Superman. Now go to sleep.' I went softly towards the stairs, past David's room.

'Don't stay up too late for Claire.'

'Thank you.'

'They're at the party.'

'Would you like me to come and bandage the rest of you?'

I looked at David's room, the photographs, the books.

'I'm going to get a drink,' I called firmly, 'and go to bed. Now sleep tight.' There was silence. I went slowly down the stairs towards the drink, glowing with my earlier exertions, and tired. I'd sleep well tonight.

'What about Claire and Andy,' Stefanie piped from her bed. 'Aren't *they* doing anything?'

'Good *night*, Steffie.'

THE WIND AND rain lulled me to sleep, but not deeply enough. In the early hours two pairs of drunken footsteps woke me as they clambered up the stairs, their authors hushing one another in whispers that would have filled the Albert Hall. I turned over, determined to remain immune. But it was futile; outside the window a misty garden appeared as the sudden file of light from Claire's window stretched out across the wet grass.

Over my drink, before going to bed, I'd put on the record player to defy the silence. Old dodderer with foggy, foggy dew, rather than Schubert. I thought of Sue singing her folk songs in Colchester, on the university campus, she'd said. Chrissie and I had attended many such concerts, holding hands in smoky halls, among the beer drinkers. I tried to make the memory my lullaby.

Instead I found myself staring at the wall, waiting for the row of photographs to shake with the activity on the other side of the partition. I shut my eyes. Could I hear bouncing? In a well-thumbed work of pornography I'd borrowed from Trevelyan at school the Edwardian heroine, after a surfeit of elegant foreplay, cried, *'Stab me, man! This is more than I can bear, or stand!'* I had pointed out the phrase to Trev, who developed a habit of saying the second part of it, with a smirk at me, while interrogating small schoolboy offenders. I groaned. President Kennedy, gazing from the wall, agreed; this was more than a man could bear, or stand. I stuffed my head into my pillow, I made erotic plans for Chrissie's first night home, it was no use; light on now, wide awake, but *Myths Of The World* only offered me Tantric couples wreathed in foolish other-worldly smiles, Oriental Cheshire cats.

I turned the page. Warlike heroes, dressed for battle in pleated skirts. One bearded captain, on a Greek vase, had an air of David; his enemies fled from him along a strip cartoon of Hell. I read: *the sacred hero, half man, half god, son of Zeus or Poseidon, is perhaps, as one commentator has suggested, simply the son of 'God-knows-whom': that is to say he was begotten at the solstice when priestesses coupled with votaries in the darkness of a sacred cave and any ensuing paternity remained in every sense a mystery.* In a cave. Ba-ba-born in a cave.

In the morning the rain had gone, but the day was gloomy. Dark clouds, driven before a blustery wind, kept us indoors. We made a poor foursome; Andy was a silent hulk—he and Claire formed a pair in a peculiarly indifferent and wordless, yet permanent manner. They sat together hand in hand on the sofa, like two strangers handcuffed together, while Steffie showered us brightly with games. Sue remained mysteriously absent. I won, with some ease, at Monopoly and Pick-A-Stick. I told silly stories, and Claire laughed. I beat Andy at ludo. Chess he refused.

I asked about his sporting activities and found to my surprise that he was an archer; but it explained his legs, which were weedy compared to his torso.

'Jack cycled all the way from London,' Claire said.

Andy grunted, and I felt ashamed.

When the weather calmed in the late afternoon I took a walk down to the beach, more to escape from Steffie's umpiring than from the way Claire was playing me off against her boyfriend. It was no contest; he was eighteen and awkward with it. We were all becoming childish.

By the windmill, where a tall shingle bank hid the sea from view, I recognized one of the parked cars. It was the Triumph. I climbed up onto the bank, and felt the full force of the wind. Darkness was coming fast, but I could see Sue in the distance, walking. I hurried after her, stumbling on the smooth stones, past fishing boats drawn high onto the beach. Their hulls were dark and pitted, and their rigging clanked like haunted battlements as I passed beneath them. I called, and called again, and Sue turned, waiting for me.

I stopped before her, panting. She kissed me on the cheek and smiled at me. 'Alone again.' I nodded. She glanced at the sky and down again, in mock despair. 'I thought you'd make it this time.'

'Andy's back. The lout,' I said unkindly. I took Sue's arm and we patrolled the shoreline. I told her about Mrs Langley. 'In other words Sindacombe's for real, as far as I can see,' I said. 'So much for that. I suppose there are people who look identical. Bad teeth and all.'

She didn't seem to be listening; or perhaps she disagreed. But surely there *were* people who looked identical, or at least astonishingly similar. Yes of course there were. In fact—and it seemed odd that this recollection had taken so long to surface—I'd always been vulnerable to resemblances, and for the first few weeks at boarding school I'd imagined myself to be surrounded by twins: pairs of vaguely similar strangers I simply hadn't learnt to tell apart. It took months before the last, obstinate pair resolved into their identifying differences, and the experience left me hesitant, long after leaving school. If I glimpsed an acquaintance in an unexpected place, I tended to assume for safety's sake (and even at the risk of causing offence) that their similarity to the person I knew was purely in my head. I was about to say so to Sue, when I noticed the contradiction: I'd done just the opposite with the man in the lane. Without hesitation, I took him for Bromley.

'Talking of errant husbands...' Sue said, studying the North Sea.

'You've heard from him?'

'He didn't get the job.' Sue paused. 'Says it was rigged, of course. Already pencilled in for some internal candidate.' She shrugged, and we walked on.

'When's he coming back?' There was a silence. 'Sue?'

'How *could* it have been rigged?' she said. 'Good grief, they flew him over there.'

'Make it *look* right,' I mumbled. 'I suppose.' Sue was wrapped in her thoughts.

'You know,' she paused. 'At one point, it must have been some time last year, he told me he was beginning to think his work here was coming to an end.'

'No kidding.' It made him sound like Billy Graham. 'Meaning what? The farm?'

Sue shook her head. 'You don't have to come here to raise pigs. It's Mission Europe we're talking about.' She checked herself. 'It's an honourable tradition: the Idaho kid tells Europe why the lights are going out. Trouble is, it's a bit like trying to explain to the old folks at home why they are the way they are. Parents, I mean. At some point you have to back up, turn around, head down the track and get on with your own life.'

'Take me with you,' I said, and was treated to a tender look. We had reached a group of little skiffs, their metal stays rattling against the mast. It was a softer sound, almost melodic. We stood by them for a while. 'Sounds just like Bromley's goats.'

Sue nodded. After a moment she gave me a puzzled look. 'What does?'

'The jangling.' I indicated the boats. Sue watched me, unusually intent. 'He's got some goat bells,' I explained, 'proper ones, from Greece. They make the same sound.' She smiled politely and turned back to the sea.

'D'you have any feelings about your father?' she said.

'How d'you mean? He's dead.'

'That's what I'm getting at.' She turned to me. 'How old were you when he died?'

'Four? Five?' I said. 'Thereabouts.' This answer echoed down the years, I used it to deflect the same old words of sympathy, the ritual condolences. It often worked; my unanticipated vagueness threw a spanner in the works.

But now another echo had been jarred into motion: good old Diophantes. Five years after his marriage was born a son; was born a son, who died five years . . . or was it four . . . and suddenly a different set of digits came into my mind: 1948. If that was the year my father died—and why else had it flashed into my head?—then I was only three years old at most. Was that right? Was it possible that I'd muddied the whole issue so much I didn't even know any more? Sue was watching me, waiting for my attention. Now she gave an apologetic smile.

'Look. How's this? We all have two fathers. Okay?' She paused to see if I was catching on. 'The one who steals Mummy. And the nice man who dandles you on his knee.'

I nodded, trying to attend. Two fathers.

I couldn't yet see what she was getting at, but whatever it was, it explained why she had seemed so indifferent, just now, to my Bromley-conclusions. With Mrs Langley's help she had been proved right all along about Bromley, but no, she wasn't content with coincidence theory, she had consistently treated me as if I was withholding something, as though the problem lay in me.

Only there was nothing *to* withhold. Yes, I'd regarded Bromley as a kind of father-substitute at boarding school, someone to woo;

nothing very mysterious in that. Now Sue was letting me into the picture as she saw it—dimestore Freud, David would say, I suspected—which involved . . . what? A two-faced Daddy who went behind your back to cuddle Mummy. Anatomically, this was becoming hard to visualize. Especially given Mother's beachball frame.

'We have to get the two together,' Sue was saying, 'as we grow up. Learn to imagine the man the way he was before he was a father. See him as a brother, if you like, a contemporary. A friend.'

'Aha,' I said. 'Well, I don't need an analyst, if I've got you. Isn't that what your woman said? Your therapist?'

Sue nodded, smiling. 'It's the friend speaking,' she agreed.

Her beady gaze belied it. 'All right,' I said. 'I'm not stupid. Bromley's Bromley. He lives in Wales. I couldn't care less.'

'Okay then.' She seemed pleased. 'Never mind him. What about marriage?'

'Marriage is bunk,' I said. 'Is that what you want to hear?'

She took my arm and we walked on across the shingle. Thinking about it I realized I meant what I'd said. Marriage was ludicrous; certainty flooded in; I knew. I'd known for years—yes, the whole idea of proposing to Chrissie had surely been designed for this: to make the overly-familiar strange and new again, to see it, right in front of me: David and Sue, Bromley and Laura, even Claire and Andy, chafing at their handcuffs, Sindacombes and Bromleys all of them. Sue made as if to speak, then stopped. I glanced at her. 'Nothing important,' she shook her head.

'About Bromley?' There was an excitement rising in me. This was a turning point, a conversation to remember.

Sue nodded, with a flick of her eyes in my direction, as to an improved pupil. 'In a sense. David thinks there's always much more going on in people's lives than we suppose. Affairs and such. I always think there's less.' She paused. '*Much* less.'

'That's because you've got such a suspicious mind,' I said.

'Me? Surely the opposite.'

'No,' I said, convinced I'd glimpsed a higher theorem; I knew there was a logic in it, although for the moment I'd lost the thread. I was feeling good, feeling as I had in the old days with Sue, talking, arguing, on the threshold of great thoughts. I wanted Sue to sense this too. 'I've got it!' I said. '*You* think there's much less going on—because you *suspect* so much *more* than anybody else does!' She laughed and we strode on towards a distant rowboat. The lights of Blakeney were coming on, in the distance.

'Do you still love David?' I asked carefully. Sue didn't pause.

'Sure I love him.' I went on watching her.

'I have a theory,' I said. 'Men are immoralists. By nature.' She was grinning; I could see she found this sort of thing too jejune to feel patronized by it. But I was in earnest. 'Women are the moralists—apparently,' I stressed. 'In fact, it's men who take it seriously. Women are in practice utterly amoral. They only *talk* morality.'

I couldn't judge Sue's expression, but her grimace seemed to be for the wind, not me. 'David speaking,' she said.

'No. That's my own.'

'It's crap,' she said indifferently, tolerant.

'It's not. What's more, morality was probably invented by men.'

Sue stopped by the rowboat and turned her face out of the wind. I could see she was smiling at me. 'So that they could break it,' she said.

'Exactly. *They* take the responsibility.'

I climbed into the rowboat, exhilarated, and sat cross-legged in the bows. Behind me the crash of the breakers came out of the gloom. Sue peered at me. 'I'm a Sufi,' I said.

'If you say so, Jack.'

I folded my legs further, in a mock lotus, trying to charm her out of her resistance. 'Bloody painful, I can tell you.'

'D'you love *me*?'

I sat in silence. 'Of course.' I couldn't see her face as clearly as I wanted. 'A little bit anyway,' I said.

'I want to sleep with you, you know that, don't you?' She brushed the hair out of her eyes. I watched her, reaching in vain for a joke about amorality, but my heart wasn't in it. 'Do I?'

'Of course you do.' She walked along next to the boat until she was beside me, then leaned in. We kissed. Sue drew back again. More than excitement, I felt the logic of it. And I was dizzy with anticipation. 'Come on,' she said, and gave me her hand to help me clamber out.

We stood smiling. I was hunting for a way of referring to her therapist's advice, to let her know that I was perfectly happy to be a part of this. There was no need. 'Doctor's orders,' said Sue. 'But I take full responsibility.'

THE COTTAGE APPEARED to be empty, as we entered the hall. There was silence. Sue squeezed my hand and signalled me to stay there, as she looked into the sitting room. The lights were on. I stood in the hall, trying not to think. Affairs were one thing; for all my talk about immorality, the mentor's wife was quite another. Through the half-open door I saw Sue walk towards the kitchen, and stop.

'Where's Andy?' she said, her back to me.

Claire's voice came from the kitchen beyond her. 'I took him to the bus.' I heard the sounds of washing up. 'Have you seen Jack?'

Sue made some sort of gesture at me, behind her back. 'Charming,' I breathed.

'Andy could have stayed,' Sue was saying. 'I don't mind.' I saw that her hand was waving at me with a meaning: I was to scuttle up the stairs. I stood my ground. I wasn't having any of this bedroom square-dance. Claire appeared briefly in the kitchen doorway. I hesitated, trying unsuccessfully to clear my face. She hadn't seen me;

I stepped back and sat on the stairs.

'No, he had to get back,' Claire said, 'he's got football tomorrow.'

'Steffie gone to bed early?' Sue asked.

'No.' I heard Claire moving across the sitting room floor. 'I'll go and see, I don't know what she's up to.'

'That's all right,' said Sue warningly, but Claire had already reached the doorway beside me. She stared at me, and glanced back at Sue. I looked with interest at the cigarette I had begun to roll. Claire stepped round and past me, and went quickly up the stairs.

I came into the sitting room, where Sue gave an unladylike chuckle at my expression. We stood listening to Claire's quick steps on the floor above. I looked down under Sue's gaze, and licked the cigarette paper. I sealed it and lit up. The silence that had fallen in the car, on the way home, resumed; there was something in Sue's manner that I hadn't expected, that I didn't associate with her, before our clinch. A kind of glad passivity: it seemed alien to her personality. Perhaps it was the American way of sex, though this wasn't the way I'd imagined it. For once, we hadn't talked much, on the way back up the beach. It had been difficult to find a subject. I'd raised bookshop business and Sue had indulged me without comment, agreeing on all counts. Then the wordless drive back, letting the nervousness settle. Words were necessary now.

From her face I could see she knew it too. 'I've fancied you for so long,' she said cheerfully.

'News to me.'

'In a pig's ear,' she said, abandoning her English phrasebook. 'You knew all along.'

'I did not,' I said. 'It wouldn't have occurred to me.' This was too pious; but I couldn't stop. 'I thought you were my big sister.'

Sue gave me a dry look. 'I'm all sorts of things,' she said. I nodded. We hadn't specified one in particular, but there was no way round it.

'Would you tell him?'

'Don't be silly. Will you?'

I grinned uncomfortably back. 'I'm sure he'd expect me to,' I said. 'He'll want all the details. The du*htails*,' I corrected. Our tenses, too, were all at sea. I was wrong, words were a mistake.

'You'd tell him?'

I thought about it. 'No, I certainly wouldn't. I certainly would not.' We stood looking at each other. Claire's footsteps retraced their way across the ceiling, and stopped. A door shut. 'I'm not up to this, Sue,' I said, and looked to her for help. Her tender, waiting gaze didn't alter, as though we could just forget I'd spoken. 'David talks about you all the time. I talk to him. It's hopeless,' I said.

'You'll be better informed.' I couldn't move. 'Don't you want me?' she said gently. I did. I made to step forward, but her eyes stayed on my face, and I didn't move. 'Oh go to hell,' she said in a more familiar tone of voice, and broke past me out of the door and up the stairs.

I stood for a while, composing myself. Despite her words, I felt it wasn't over. But it was a chance to think it through again, to face up to possible repercussions. Claire as hostile witness, David flying back defeated. Lord knows what he'd been up to himself—but then, never drop one in your own backyard, that was his maxim; this was his backyard, and mine; his wife, and my employer. Sue, in her turn, slammed a door, upstairs. The more I thought about it, the angrier I got with Thurgo friend and listener. I'd been Trevelyan's tool too long. I owed it to myself. There were two women, waiting. *Stab me, man!* A third set of footsteps, mine, stormed up the stairs.

I lingered in David's study, for tempers to cool and Steffie's bedroom light to go out, restoring a strip of the garden to semi-obscurity. Three more runways of light remained, including mine. Doors shut again, the house went still. I looked once more at Kennedy and Kerouac, remembering last night. One of the snaps seemed even more appropriate: young David in the Indonesian jungle, wearing a safari suit but no shirt, with either arm round a hideous, diminutive, bare-breasted woman; the breasts sagged, neither small nor quality, and the smiling pygmy faces were pitted with scars. David looked every inch the happy conqueror. His shameless grin announced America—it wouldn't have done for the *National Geographic*, but it could have fronted *Henderson The Rain King*. The complete Bellow lined the shelves. I drummed on the desk. Was it love or lust, boy? Lust, sir, I smiled into the headmaster's face, and turned to stride from the room, expelled with honour.

At the far end of the corridor, Sue's door was ajar. I walked softly, and stopped at Claire's bedroom. As I pressed the door handle it squeaked for all the house to hear. I pushed quickly to enter, and fell against the door. It was locked. 'Claire?' I whispered.

A singsong voice came from the end room and its open door.

'Oh no you don't,' it sang.

I tried the door in front of me once more, in vain; no footsteps came to let me in.

'Locked out?' came Sue's voice again.

I walked down to her doorway, slowly. Sue posed on the bed, over a book, still dressed, her look all innocence. I leaned against the door jamb and shrugged. Sue chuckled, and beckoned with a forefinger. I stayed where I was. 'Just what have you two been up to?' I said. 'Is this a combined operation?'

Sue shook her head. 'We're not *all* amoral,' she said, 'that's all.' She lay back on the bed, black hair spread. Her trousered legs sprawled on the bedcover.

I came to the bed, inhaling. It was the perfume again, filling the room. The bedhead and the coverlet showed dainty flowers; Sue lay indelicately on them, lazy legs apart. I sat on the bed, leaning over her, and kissed her. There was no movement from her. I kissed her

134

again, and her mouth opened to receive my tongue, like a warm bowl of milk. I kissed the breath out of her, and drew back. Her soft, full arms were still; I touched her hand; it yielded, warm but limp. Her face gave me no signal. The mouth half open, breathing heavily from the kiss, the eyes wide, a submissive calf. We kissed some more. I began to undo her blouse. Breasts freckled from the sun came into view. The blouse peeled back. I worked with both arms around her broad chest, fingers underneath her, feeling for the bra straps; it was like wrestling with a beach ball. Sue giggled.

'The door,' she breathed, and I turned furtively, my face in her glorious, fragrant breasts. The doorway was empty; I climbed off my tethered steer and went to the door. This seemed to spring her into action: in seconds flat she had wriggled off the blouse and stripped away the bra, shaking her shoulders proudly. Her hair swung, and with it her breasts. I felt sorry for pygmy warriors. The huge aureoles stood out like targets against the paler skin. The delicious ritual began. Sue stood up, beside the bed, and took her trousers off. I stood by the door, hurrying, several articles behind. As she removed her panties I dropped my clothes in a heap onto a chair. Sue smiled, waiting for me. If I had anticipated a moment of unfamiliarity, of nervousness before her, it never came. To my surprise Sue naked was no more physical than Sue clothed. And no less; I had bathed in her warmth for so many years. But it was disconcerting. I looked her splendid body up and down, waiting for the shock of nudity. It came, but faintly. I felt positively marital.

I walked to her, and we embraced. We fitted perfectly. For a moment it was confusingly, absurdly chaste, like a goodnight kiss. Then to my relief I felt my body respond, vigorously. So did Sue. I pushed her back towards the bed, still tight against her in a crablike dance, but this was better than the waltz with Washington. We toppled onto the bed, happily, and squirmed into position. I lay on top of her, ready, her smiling, friendly face beneath mine. I gazed at her, measuring the moment. Until now, her mild though glad expression had helped to bridge the introductory movement. At this point I could have done with some Edwardian boudoir cries, but it was not to be. This was clearly what she could bear, or stand, all night. And so could I; I decided I was well rid of the spice of guilt.

She was warm and wet, and as ready as I was. I entered her and rode in silence; she watched me, smiling away, as though pleased to be of service. I began to wonder whether I was doing something wrong. Perhaps a few rodeo slaps, a yell or two. I was gratified by her smile, but all the same I wasn't quite sure of the place of humour during sex. Before and after was another matter. Chrissie was an ardent moaner, during; and for all I knew an ardent liar, but it was thoroughly encouraging. I drove harder at Sue. She never flinched. I felt as if I could go on all night like this, erect into eternity. I wondered where we went from here, and kissed her violently to smother the glad expression.

It was all going extremely well, without going anywhere in particular, and I couldn't switch off my mind. Perhaps we'd rushed the foreplay. Should I turn her over? It was a daunting prospect. Even with Chrissie I'd found the operation perilously comical. Perhaps the bed was the wrong place to be; but we were firmly in and on the bed, as the valley of bedclothes bore witness. I rammed on, as sweat began to trickle down between us, producing wallowing sounds. There must be something constrained, I reflected, about the first fuck, something predictably conventional. Perhaps the thing to do was to get it over with. Certainly Chrissie and I had taken months to admit and refine our tastes. I focused on Sue's wobbling breasts, caressed them and licked them appreciatively. They were a treat; but the end was still far from sight. I struggled not to think of Claire. At last Sue made a sound, although it might have been discomfort. I didn't care. It spurred me towards a climax and with its approach my confidence revived. I was the master here; I'd show her. Streaks of sensation rushed towards my groin from every part, my eyelids shut, starfire replaced Sue's face, and I shouted, triumphant.

When I opened my eyes at last, her smile was even broader. She spoke for the first time. 'More,' she said, in Steffie's greedy voice.

In time, we did more. And I surpassed myself in sheer endurance. But Sue's friendly manner remained. I couldn't work out what it was that might unlock something different in her, something less easygoing. I felt I would receive the same contented acquiescence if I suggested we did it hanging from the churchyard trees. Maybe there was no secret trigger, no frenzy to be released. Why should there be? She seemed to be deriving pleasure. But where had all the anger gone, the anger that seemed to be contained, with effort, by her daily personality? I wondered if my disappointment was unworthy, only a tiresome puritanical quest for a bit of dirt. Maybe this was New World sex, service with a smile. It wasn't so much an initiation that I wanted, a Bacchanalia, that wasn't really in my line. I wanted a promotion. A new intimacy. A secret Sue, for myself.

I had a fancy for her breasts, and tried to put it into action, sliding myself carefully between them. Chrissie's were nearer to Claire's in size and rating, and these great pliant globes were a new experience. But the idea proved more vivid than the execution; I slid in vain, and Sue took me forgivingly into her mouth.

Between bouts I did the talking, and Sue lay back, watching me tenderly. I told stories of school, of Trev, and 'Tosser' Williamson, renowned for his consecutive achievements. On one famous occasion he had been practising on a milk bottle, when the bell for prayers rang. Engorged, he found himself stuck in the bottle and had to shut his flies over it and hurry down to assembly. Ten minutes later the Lord's Prayer was accompanied by the smash of a bottle, which appeared out of his trouser leg and splintered at his feet. Sue laughed delightedly and pulled me back on top of her.

She was relentless. It was a blissful candy feast; peanut butter and jelly sandwiches until I burst. The dawn chorus sang us to sleep.

I WAS ALONE in the enormous bed when I woke up, and it was late. I gazed round. The bed itself was so much larger than any I was used to, and the furnishings, with their matching chintzes, belonged to another world; a world I was at ease in by right of a privileged education and my mother's labours—like the church outside Sue's window I was styled on the proceeds of wool. But it was not the world I lived in, this spacious, well-upholstered place. I merely liked to peep into it, as in a crystal. Highgate basements, Hammersmith flats were my habitat, though Chrissie's parents would no doubt endow us with chintzes—the thought was out before I could check it, or remember what I'd declared the night before, on the beach, about marriage; somehow the night had dissipated all conviction.

I rolled across the princely sheets and set down my feet on carpet. I felt a fine tiredness, dry, scoured of emotion—that was it, scoured as a pan—and satisfied with my lot. No twinges of guilt; there was nothing of David in the room. It was utterly Sue's domain, and I felt proud of conquest, free to leave. It was heady. I went to the window and looked out possessively at the familiar scene. The clouds had gone, leaving a long overdue freshness to the day. My bicycle shone as if new, beside the hedge. Then I recalled the wobbling of the wheels; I groaned, but secretly I saw myself hefting the bike into the guard's van of the train, reprieved. Out of the corner of my eye I noticed movement. The sketchbook protuded from the next window along, a slim hand working on the page. I drew back.

Downstairs I found Sue, dressing-gowned, eating her breakfast at the kitchen table. Steffie was sitting on the steps to the garden, levering the tortoise up and over them like a toy tractor. They both gave me a cheery smile, and Sue rose to make me some food. I could see no second thoughts in her eyes; everything was all right; even Steffie seemed oddly serene. I sat casually at the table. No words passed, no secret looks, as if my late appearance needed none. I felt like father.

'Eggs?' said Sue.

'Lovely.'

I felt at home; it was absurd. As the eggs sizzled in the pan Sue came and kissed me softly on my crown. Steffie wasn't looking, preoccupied with her toy. But there was nothing to see, after all. Two friendly people. I began to worry—was this meant to be a beginning? I'd had my feast: now for immersion.

'How d'you like them?' Sue asked, stirring the eggs. She glanced at me. No, there was nothing but the old relationship in her look. I felt ashamed at my suspicions.

'Over-easy.'

Smiling, Sue shook her head, 'Too late, they're scrambled,' and dished them up. She sat down opposite me as I ate. Her stare was tender, but she gauged the atmosphere well, it was reassuring, too. She glanced out into the sunlit garden. 'I thought we might go to the beach today,' she said.

'Yippee,' went Steffie, dropping the tortoise. It clattered on the bricks, indifferent, protected.

'With Stefanie on a lead,' said Sue sternly, adding, 'I wish you wouldn't bounce that animal.'

'At some point,' I said, 'I think I'd better head back.'

'Oh?' Sue looked at me.

'No...' Steffie wheedled.

'You pick up that tortoise,' I said, 'and apologize.'

She did, shouting 'Sorry, tortoise!' into its dark, gaping shell. '*Now* will you stay?'

I shrugged. 'There may be news waiting,' I said, and hesitated to mention from whom. 'It's been a week.'

Sue nodded, motherly. 'Come to the beach.'

'I ought to go.'

'Not yet,' she said. 'At least say hello to David.'

'David?' said Steffie. Sue nodded, still looking at me. 'Yay,' went the child happily, as before, but this time without dropping the tortoise: I felt the beach and I held the edge in her affections.

'When's he due?' I wasn't at all sure about this idea.

Sue shrugged, and for the first time this morning something veiled her eyes. 'He's back,' she said. 'Arrived last night.'

I stared at her and let my fork down to my plate. Sue couldn't hold my gaze, and looked away. 'Last night?' I said, incredulous. I felt numb. He was here? But where? Upstairs? I gaped. The study! Or . . . Claire's room? 'Here?'

'What?' Sue looked at me, amazed, and then recovered with a soundless laugh. 'Not in the house, you fool. In London. He's coming today.'

'Goody,' said Steffie firmly, to make sure she was in on whatever was going on. I was still staring at Sue. She knew, yesterday. Last night. She'd had news, she'd known. I nodded, pushing my plate away. Well then, this was no beginning. So much the better. I would leave at once.

'Go and play,' said Sue, turning to Steffie. 'Take that thing back to its bush.' The girl eyed us, and went, smiling.

I stood and took my plate to the sink, pressing it under the water. 'Jack, you can't go now, just as he gets here,' Sue said. 'What will he think?'

'Think what he likes. Tell him my mother's been kidnapped by a diabolic cult.' I wiped the plate clean.

'Jack, please,' she said. 'For me.'

'Why are we going to the beach, then, if he's on his way?'

'Because. There's no need for a welcoming committee. I really don't know when he's coming.'

'Won't he ring? I mean, from the station or something? There'll be no-one here.'

140

Sue didn't answer. She came and took the plate from me, to dry it. 'He'll take a taxi,' she shrugged. She put the plate away and walked to the doorway, watching Steffie bury the tortoise in the foliage. 'To give you some idea of the state of things,' she said, 'he won't have told you but he's had his driving licence removed, and d'you know what? He won't let me drive him,' she turned back, 'because *I'm* such a lousy driver!'

'He's right,' I said, 'you are.'

She turned her eyes to heaven, and laughed. 'I think you'd better stay, you two have so much in common.' I glanced at her, but there was only humour in her eyes. 'Don't worry, we'll go to the beach and have a nice time and Claire will tell him where we are. I think she wants to be on her own a bit, anyway.'

I watched her. 'You want Claire to tell him what we're up to?'

'Oh come on,' said Sue. 'She'll tell him we're on the beach, that's all.' She turned back to the garden. 'You don't understand her.' I raised my hands in surrender; this was all quite new to me. 'Stef!' she called.

I went upstairs to fetch my trunks, while Sue prepared some sandwiches, with Steffie's help. The study brought home David's impending presence to me, but I felt less troubled than I'd feared. It really was as if nothing had happened. Sue and I hadn't said a word about last night, and the peculiar thing was that this didn't seem like a guilty forbearance. It didn't even feel like tact; we never so much as hinted at it with our eyes. It was last night's experience all over again: nothing was changed by it. The relief was unnerving. I took my trunks and left the room. Of all things, to feel cheated of shame!

As I walked to the stairs, a fist rapped on the front door and I froze.

David wouldn't knock, or would he, to create an entrance? I could hear Sue coming heavily through the sitting room. I stood, preparing myself, and feeling a welcome tension rise. My motives were all over the place; but I didn't want it to be so easy, so meaningless, to greet David again after what had happened. I watched as Sue approached and opened the door, without readying herself and without a glance up the stairs at me. She was doing it right, of course. But I couldn't move to join her. Her body brought to mind a jumble of remembered poses.

'Oh,' said Sue below me, sounding startled. 'Hello.'

A voice came from beyond the doorway, a voice rich in East Anglian melody.

'Would you by any chance be Mrs 'Ardin'?'

I relaxed. From where I stood I couldn't see who it was, but I didn't think David's East Anglian accent was good enough for the impersonation.

'Yes, that's right,' said Sue. There was a moment's pause. 'How are you?'

'Middlin' thank you,' came the voice, 'I was out of my bed for the fust time as yest'dy.' The voice. I felt myself begin to tingle. I couldn't believe it.

Sue turned and glanced up at me. A half smile had formed on her lips; it grew as she saw my expression. She turned quickly back. 'Come in,' she said.

No-one came into sight. 'I don't want to bother you, but I believe you came to my assistance,' sang the voice, a downwards cadence, 'in the road, there.'

'Well, not really,' said Sue. 'Look—do come in...'

The boater with the blue band bobbed inside the doorway. I couldn't see the face beneath it, but I saw the familiar suit, the fancy waistcoat. I stood, rigid, on the landing.

'I wanted to thank you,' said the man. 'I hope you don't mind, I got the address from the lady at the hospital.' Sue nodded and looked up at me. I barely took her in; the man had followed her gaze and was smiling at me, hopeful. 'There's a Mr Thurgo stayin', I was told,' he stared up at me for confirmation, 'a Mr Thurgo stayin' with

Mrs 'Ardin'.'

The face was innocent. Sindacombe's face. But why had he emphasized those words? *Stayin'* with *Mrs 'Ardin'*. Hadn't he emphasized them? And the leer in the voice. I glanced at Sue—surely she'd heard it—and back at the insistent, interrogative face. Bromley's face.

'Yes,' Sue was saying, 'yes, this is Jack.'

The man smiled. 'Come to see me in the hospital. Against the rules, they said.'

'That's right, yes.' Sue cupped her hand impatiently at me, to come down.

'How d'you do?' said the man. I came down the stairs and stopped above the bottom step, keeping my distance. This time I was going to handle it my way.

'Arthur Sindacombe,' he said, and removed his hat, stepping into the hall.

SUE USHERED US into the sitting room; our visitor declined to sit down. He stood. We all stood, and Steffie looked on from the kitchen doorway.

'He was the one who found you,' Sue said, indicating me.

'I remember that, you see. I do remember that.' He eyed me shyly. I bided my time; after all, it was a glorious performance, Bromley's masterpiece. The hair slicked down, face shining, watch-chain twinkling. And the dialect, polished in Cromer pubs. 'I don't remember you t' see to, though,' he said, 'but I remember someone gettin' a hold of me as I was goin' to fall. I've never felt so queer.' He smiled round at each of us in turn, noting the little girl. 'How do,' he nodded. 'I reckon I'd've hurt myself, Jack, if you hadn't 'a caught me—stumblin' around, I was, like a dog with three legs, dot an' carry one, thass what we call it when a person's had a few too many, shall we say!' He beamed. 'Lucky to be alive at all. If that door hadn't gone to open, eh? Threw me clean out into the road, or I'd've fetched up dead.'

'Yes, that was lucky,' said Sue brightly.

'Yes that was, that was. I might have fetched up dead.' He laughed, shaking his head.

A silence fell. The man was looking round the room, with nothing more to say, embarrassed. Oh, the accent was too good; too good, too rich, but I was having to fight to hold on to my certainty. Sue sat, and gestured at another chair. 'Please...'

'No thank you, no, I won't stay,' he murmured. 'Jack,' he was shy once more, 'I'm ever s' grateful to you.' He placed the boater on an armrest and extended a hand.

'That's all right.'

He grinned round, hand still outstretched. 'This time I won't fall over, look.' The gentle, downward-falling song. Sue and Steffie laughed. I had no choice, and took his hand. Firm; hard; Bromley's.

'Mummy! The eggs...' called Steffie in sudden alarm.

Sue rose quickly. 'I'm preparing a picnic,' she said, moving towards the kitchen. 'Would you like something? Something to drink?'

He shook his head, and let me go. After a swift look at my face he ambled after Sue, towards the kitchen. 'No matters,' he smiled, 'you just carry on.' Then, with his second glance at me, my doubts vanished. 'That's a nice place you've got here.' Why else were the look, the words, directed at me? 'That is a nice place.' He nodded at the gadget-crammed kitchen, at Sue attending to the eggs. 'All manner o' what!' Happy ghost, eh, Thurgo? The glance was gleeful. Got a good woman, Thurgo? *Whose* woman?!

Steffie was still in the doorway. She saw my expression, and made it hers, fixing the man with a Gestapo stare.

'We're goin' on a proper holiday,' he announced. 'Make a better go of it this time.'

I turned quickly to the window. The car; the totty. I couldn't see anything at first, but when I moved to it the view revealed a bright new Volvo, further down the curb. In it a girl with bobbed hair, sitting at the wheel.

'You're going back to Cromer?' Sue called from the cooker.

'Oh no. No, I don't think so. What shall I say . . . we don't have very happy memories of Cromer. Not now.'

I'll say, Johnny, I thought, and turned to advance on him.

'You'll be wantin' to be shunt of me,' he said, seeing me coming. 'I won't keep you.'

'No. You've done very well,' I said. He gave me a puzzled look. 'Recovering so fast.'

'Well, I en't fully recovered. Only just got out of bed.'

'Really?' I held the pause. 'I'm glad you dropped in. Very glad. You had me worried for a time.' My tone was making him stare. 'You left the hospital so suddenly...' I explained. Two could play at this game.

'Yes . . . my wife . . .' he trailed away. Sue had appeared behind Steffie. I ignored her signals.

'I'd like to meet her,' I said, nodding at the window and the car beyond. 'Is that her, in the driving seat? Do ask her to come in.'

'Well I would, Jack, but we're a little short of time.'

'I'm sure you are. You'd better hurry, hadn't you, or you'll be late for the show.'

'Jack . . .' came Sue's voice warningly.

The man glanced at her. 'Is there a show round here?'

'Not far,' I said. 'At Diss. A goat show—so you said.'

In the pause, he looked from Sue to me, blankly.

'Stop it,' Sue hissed at me.

The blank expression darkened. 'What's the matter?' he said. 'Did I say somethin' wrong?'

Stefanie gave a giggle. 'You're Bromley,' she said.

He turned to her. 'Beg pardon?'

I smiled at Steffie. 'Yes,' I said. 'You are, aren't you.' His mouth was open. I looked pleasantly at him. 'I know who you are, John. You don't fool me.'

But I was wasting my charm. He was a picture of incomprehension.

'I'm sorry,' said Sue, 'it's the child, she's just having a game. Don't mind them, Mr Sindacombe.' She met my angry gaze, unyielding.

'I see . . . yes . . .' he mumbled, and bent over Stefanie, the kindly, stooping uncle. 'Am I . . . am I interferin' with somethin'?'

'Why don't you go away?' I said. 'You don't fool us.'

'Shut up!' Sue snapped and turned to Stefanie, pulling her back into the kitchen. 'That's quite enough from you.' She rounded on me next. 'It's only a game. Isn't it.'

'Is it hell a bloody game!' I said. There was a silence.

Bromley—oh it was Bromley, to the last yellow tooth—was giving a fine impression of a stranger caught in crossfire. Sue took it out on Steffie, but I knew her anger was for me.

'You'll apologize to Mr Sindacombe,' she told the child. 'Won't you.' But Steffie's loyal face was set firm. Sue's voice trembled. 'Steffie. I'm warning you!'

It was going all wrong. 'Look,' I said, 'perhaps I—'

'Well, I'd best be off,' said my tormentor, absently. 'Ever s' thankful,' he murmured, and smiled at me.

'Please,' I begged. 'Just once. John.'

The old boy twisted his face into a grimace of willingness, and looked at Sue for help. I couldn't take it any more. I brushed past him, and past Sue and Steffie, into the kitchen, and ran on down the steps onto the grassy bricks.

'I'm sorry,' came Sue's voice. 'I'd better tell you the truth.' I strode off down the garden, my eyes prickling with tears, not wanting to hear her version. There wasn't far enough to escape it. 'It's simply a coincidence,' she was saying, 'you look like someone else, a friend of his. A schoolmaster.'

'I do?' came the jolly Suffolk tones.

'He thought you were pretending to be someone else, or rather that the other man was, that's why he's—he's . . .'

I shook my head at the hedge, longing for a shell like Steffie's tortoise.

'He's just upset.'

'Oh. Is 'a?' The voice was coming nearer; into the kitchen, advancing to inspect the strange young man in the garden.

'I'm so sorry. It's not your fault.'

I glanced; yes, they were both peering at me from the kitchen doorway. 'A schoolmaster?' he repeated with astonishment. Thurgo, go and stand in the corner. I looked up at Claire's window. Empty.

'It's a coincidence, that's all.'

'That must be. That *must* be.' They gazed at me. 'Well now, if you're ever in Newmarket you must come round to mine, you won't find no schoolmaster but you're welcome to come round, and bring the boy.' Amusement swelled in his voice. 'He won't find no schoolmaster! You'll do that, won't you?'

'Yes, of course.'

'Well . . . I'll say goodbye.' The voice carried to include me, if I was willing. I turned; I had to hand it to him, full marks. He gave a perfect awkward little wave. I waved politely back, controlled.

Their voices faded as they went back through the kitchen. But I wanted to see this to the end. I walked back along the hedge and made my way around the oil tank at the side of the house, to where I could see the pavement, the Volvo, and the green beyond. The girl sat patiently before the wheel—then I watched her turn, hearing footsteps, to the natty figure paddling into view. He came past, smiling at her; the jaunty walk, erect, was faultless to the last. Was he perhaps a madman, a split personality: Bromley really thinking he was Sindacombe?

There was something missing. I couldn't place it for a moment. Then I saw. The hat: it wasn't there. He too had registered its absence, as though at the same instant, and turned. Other footsteps came, running lightly. Stefanie held up the boater. 'You left your hat,' she said.

If I hoped for a momentary lapse in concentration, now that the fun was over, it never came. 'Thank you,' he said, 'that's bran' new, my wife give it to me an' I will keep forgettin' it. Give me everlastin' trouble, that do.'

My heart sank. It bore out Mrs Langley's story all too well. Could they really be two men, two people? In a flash it occurred to me that Bromley, of course, would have left the hat deliberately. For me; a signal. The inheritor. *Stayin' with Mrs 'Ardin', eh!* Who was to wear the boater now?

But no. No: no, it was forgetful Sindacombe, that's all. And I was mad as a teapot.

I had one staunch supporter, though. Steffie looked up at the man, with her mother's unyielding eyes. 'Lose your head next,' she said sternly, handing him the hat; and stared him into retreat.

WE SPED ONCE more into Blakeney, to the beach. Claire was still in purdah, in her room, and Sue had made no overtures, merely announcing our departure with a yell up the stairs. With Steffie hugging the sandwiches we climbed into the car and drove, in silence. I rolled a misshapen cigarette, as Sue overtook the queuing cars of more tolerant holidaymakers. Lighting it was another problem.

Sue shook her head, unable to contain herself any longer. 'All you did was embarrass the poor guy...'

We braked, and I narrowly avoided setting fire to myself.

'Sorry,' said Sue. And then, in a less irritable tone. 'Sorry, Jack.'

I got out another match. 'If you want to know, he was loving every minute of it,' I said. Inwardly, I had conceded; but I wasn't going to lose face. 'Thass a nice place you got here Jack boy,' I mimicked, with salacious undertones, 'all manner o' what har har.'

She looked at me less harshly, smiling. 'All right. Where was the famous stammer, then?'

'Just watch the road, d'you mind?' I lit the cigarette.

'Where was the stammer?'

'That's just it, Bromley never did,' I said, meeting her eyes, 'on stage.'

That *was* just it. It was true. And true that every clue—I pictured them as fine strands under the microscope—sheered neatly into two, under . . . at the touch of a razor. No, say it: under obsession's knife.

Sue was laughing. Her temper was gone. 'Ring him, then,' she was saying. 'See if he's at home.'

I shook my head. 'He's here in Norfolk, Sue, that's the whole point. He warned me—he's coming to Diss to judge a goat show.'

The joke revived, and we laughed our last remaining awkwardness away. As we walked to the beach, Steffie racing ahead of us, the barriers between us broke, even the barriers of our studied ease. We lay protected in the dunes, and Sue played skilfully with me under the sand, while Steffie paddled, cautious, and discreet, leaving us be. For both our sakes I tried to conjure David's face, in warpaint like the young Americans he spoke of in the postcard, thrusting out of a nearby tussock, to help myself discourage Sue. But she was having fun while it lasted, so was I, and Dying Buffalo, it seemed, was still roaming old London haunts, in no hurry to return. I had the postcard in my pocket; *can't find a butcher man.* I had the knife; it wasn't going to make us blood brothers.

We ate egg sandwiches, laced with sand, and talked about her childhood, spent more in New York, it seemed, than her old Virginia home. They'd drop in on the plantation by private seaplane, for the weekend. All the trappings of the unimaginably rich. And the morals, I told myself.

As Sue talked and I coloured in a strip-cartoon America, we watched her child make mud pies in the North Sea silt. Ponies, servants, five-course meals, as Sue described them, these would be part of the girlhood Steffie was entering, at Daddy's expense. Sue's first husband was a hotshot Southern lawyer. I saw him blond and handsome; rich at birth and bent on keeping it that way—'a triple Scorpio,' Sue had said grimly, an obsessive, a purebred workaholic. Worth was the name, and his was in at least seven figures, the reason, I took it, for the marriage. It was as much the lack of malice as the lack of affection, when Sue talked about him, that made me think it was no love match. Black boys waited at his table; old but far from vanished ways. The money itself wasn't new. Like my friend Trevelyan, Paul Worth senior had seen both sides of the law without losing status, or the building contracts in his native city of Richmond. While his friends were out of office Paul senior had done a spell in jail, in the Thirties, working in a road gang; a black limousine cruised every day beside the toiling men, the chauffeur handing Mr Paul his chicken sandwiches.

This story I neither believed nor disbelieved: for me there was no real America, since nothing could replace the imaginary one, not even its living facsimile however lurid. My favourite figure was Worth junior, Sue's ex-husband. Young Mr Paul had earned his chicken sandwiches a different way. A reputable law firm; his colleagues, Southern gentlemen; he himself was straight as a die. On the other hand he was crazy, crazy enough to have made David seem—I suspect—a haven of normality. I always made Sue talk about him. Conspiracy was Paul Worth's game, his hobbyhorse; not a nest of familiar bogeymen, no rag-bag of Jewish bankers, blacks, Commies or men from Mars, but one homely and all-embracing plot. Its authors were one family, the House of Orange. I could only picture stolid William and Mary on a throne built for two, but no, this evil line, pledged to the downfall of free market forces everywhere, had financed every revolution the world had ever seen. Except the American one of course, against which they had raised troops themselves—from Hesse, Liechtenstein, Bavaria, Sue knew each regiment and their secret paymaster—and sent them to fight beside the British. Facts poured from Sue to stem my laughter. Robespierre—oh yes, Robespierre—the Orange devils had paid in coin. The Russian business required more subtle promptings—to believe Paul, their London agent had personally paid Karl Marx's London laundry bills. 'Don't snigger,' Sue said sombrely, 'Paul's got the bills in his safe, and I mean the originals.'

Sue never discussed the move from Crazy Horse to Dying Buffalo. But I had my own version. David striding Greenwich Village, as I imagined him, equally passionate in his own way about a general collapse—from jazz to James Jones things were falling apart, and in their wake came rock stars and the plastic grass beneath the Houston Astrodome. Things grow chillsome, he was wont to say; but at least David didn't blame the House of Orange. And there was a remedy. He took Sue to the mountains. They climbed and camp-fired and canoed, and exorcized the world of Paul Worth. A temporary remedy; with them went despair. The land was being poisoned, less by chemicals than by consciousness: it remained a simulated frontier. Log cabin dreams faded, little by little; history, like air traffic, constantly surveyed them. And Sue, till now, had never really taken to the outdoor life. They gave up. If you couldn't beat history, you could join it. Europe beckoned—and England, queen of despair. This was not my verdict but David's. 'Any Englishman who eats well is a faggot!' he claimed, tracing even our eating habits to despair, to an honourable nihilism. 'The true Englishman eats his food filthy, cold, and preferably in his room—he knows he cannot break the bread, he needs to say grace but he knows he can't!' Alone of nations we preferred to fail the feast rather than fake it, and David loved us for it. We made the great refusal, we were endstation Culture, and we knew it.

The wind freshened as the afternoon wore on. We took a last dip and, shivering, packed to go, no longer Running Bear and Minnie-haha. Perhaps David wouldn't return at all, sensing something, or just plain reluctant to come home to Sue. The three of us hugged tight against the wind, walking back to the car, Steffie huddled between our legs. We took it slowly.

DAVID WAS IN the sitting room, reclining before a log fire, looking as if he'd never been away. We saw him through the front windows, as we pulled up in the car. 'Well, there he is,' said Sue, and Steffie banged excitedly on the car window. David watched the grate, oblivious.

A cool evening was coming on, and after the heat of the Middle West, David must have needed the fire; but it looked incongruous, it was as if we'd slipped a season, one that Sue and I had spent together. As we entered the sitting room, David was at the fireplace removing a gas-fired gadget. One of his so-called sensible technologies, firelighting without tears.

'Well now,' he scooped up Steffie in his arms, 'how was the beach?'

He looked fine, untired, the broad, curly-bearded face ruddy with sunshine. The plaid shirt and corduroy trousers were the customary uniform; he squeezed the squealing child, backwoodsman Daddy. 'Hey buns,' he smiled at me. It was an endearment; but there was none for Sue. This was not unusual, they seemed to pride themselves on a silent accord, the hunter bringing home the frozen spoils, or none, without comment, after a hard week's trapping. I found this side of him embarrassing, but my sympathy was wasted on Sue, she seemed to like it. And on this occasion I could see she wasn't going to ask about Chicago. That was my role.

'Where's Claire?' she said.

David eyed her. 'She's in her room,' he said. 'She didn't seem to require my company.' Sue hovered for a moment, impassive, then took the picnic remains into the kitchen. 'We talked awhile,' said David into the fire, 'and I pushed off downstairs again. It's *so* good to feel wanted when you get home.' He released Steffie, and patted her. I tried to see the homecoming differently; perhaps he and Sue had already broken the ground yesterday, on the phone.

'You could have come to the beach,' Sue called.

He turned to me. 'Hope you don't mind about the fire. It's going to be a long hard winter.' I believed him. He appraised me for a time, and nodded. 'Looking good,' he said, smiling.

'And you,' I said. 'But no joy from the institutional tit.'

'Well, no Chair. But they liked me so much they offered me a little hidey-hole round the back of the building. My very own broom cupboard.' Steffie giggled; David sat and took her on his knee. 'I told them to go find some broken-down Chief, let him do it.'

Sue came to the kitchen doorway. 'They offered you *what?*'

'Ol' Chief Broom's job, sweepin' the corridors.' Sue waited him out. 'Assistant Professorship,' he explained, expressionless.

'And you said *no?*'

'Guess whose job it was,' said David, turning to her. 'This is beautiful: my ol' buddy Butterworth. I only found out the story when I got there.' He turned back to avoid her stare. 'They'd kicked him out after a year, for some or other reason, too much dope with the philosophy. And now guess where he is. He's back in San Francisco, on the streets. But really on the streets.' He grinned at me. 'They tell me he's been made a ward of Alameda County. He walks the richest sidewalks in the world, talks Hegel to the winos.' He turned round once more, gleaming, to Sue. 'Me and my little pee-haitch-dee... man, he's got a *stack* of books behind him. How d'you like it? A ward of Alameda County... and *he* was *good.*'

Sue said nothing, just stared back. Upstairs a door opened, and shut again. We listened to Claire coming down the stairs. As she came in, Sue turned and went back to the kitchen. Claire entered with a smile for me and Steffie; David hadn't turned back. No-one spoke, and Claire continued through into the kitchen.

David glanced at me, bland. 'Don't you find it a little close in here? Why don't you and I take some air?'

Wrapped in a cavernous parka, David led me onto Newgate Green, where he stopped and looked up at the emerging stars. I did the same; unless you were careful, walking with David was an irritating series of fits and starts, stopping and returning to him, wrong-footed. He laughed and clapped me on the back. I was the trusted ally, or the willing tool, it scarcely mattered, all I knew was that I wasn't going to get away tonight. My thoughts went back to Claire; she'd looked composed again, clear-eyed, delectable. And I had nothing more to lose, if opportunity presented itself. In for a penny, in for a pound; sin and repent, go home refreshed, 'better informed', as Sue put it. David set off at a ferocious pace across the Green and I scurried to keep up with him, admonishing myself. The situation was troubled enough already, best leave well alone.

I glanced at him. Our walks had always been marked by comfortable silences, and I felt no differently about this one, despite my night with Sue. In fact, for the first time I felt protective towards them: what had happened to the sly, happy banter of old, David and Sue challenging all comers to match their swordsmanship? It had inspired in me a jealous awe, I longed to bottle their casual panache and take it home to study. But now the bristling, furry beast had gone into a chrysalis of silence; portending ... what? A treaty of some kind, or a sniper's war?

'Okay,' David said without slackening his stride. 'You've had your way with Mamzelle Claire and now she hates you.'

I disabused him and he halted, hands on hips.

'What the matter with you, Jackson? I mean, I hear wanking's making a comeback, but—wait a minute, didn't you get my letter?' I nodded. 'Didn't I tell you about Mamzelle?'

'Not really,' I said. 'You told me to take it easy.' I pushed the grosser ironies from my mind.

'Ha ha hee hee,' David chanted, 'Mamzelle hates *me*...'

I should have guessed; it was Sue who put me off the scent; but if he'd had his way with Claire, then I was simply Sue's revenge. Oh God. No wonder there was cordite in the air; and Trevelyan's Tool was in the firing line.

'So you didn't . . .' He left it unfinished and shook his head, muttering 'Dooby zooby' in the key of 'I'll be damned'. He walked a short way away, as though bemused.

I didn't want to dwell on it. 'How about you?' I said. 'How was Chicago?'

'Oh . . . I've had myself a time,' he smiled. Then he was striding back towards me, pointing a finger. 'I know where you've been. In the anchorite's hole!'

'Have I?' I faltered. 'What anchorite's hole?'

David nodded at the great pile looming up across the Green. 'In St Margaret's,' he said, 'up in the tower. You sure you haven't been in there, Jackson, praying for chastity?'

Inside, the huge empty church was surprisingly warm, the gloom retained some of the heat of the day, now stale and cloying, sifted from the wind by the expanses of yellow-stained glass. Ochre twilight fell on a small huddle of pews—the rest had clearly been removed to spare the blushes of a dwindling congregation, leaving in their place flagstones mottled with bird droppings. On the back of the door a plaintive notice ran, *Please keep the door shut because the birds get in,* which some vicarage helper had signed, with unconscious humour, *for the vicar.* It seemed they might have got the vicar, since the vaulted roof was alive with swallows and David acted as if he owned the church, marching up the aisle uttering cries which roused his flock from the rafters. There had been, mercifully, no mention at all of Sue, and I realized there wasn't going to be; at the moment she was not a favoured topic. I offered up a silent prayer, watching David return along the aisle, pause at the pulpit, then think better of it and walk on past. A mixture of shooby-zoobs and Hebraic Elohims filled the air—David wasn't Jewish, only a passionate Talmudist, and a vicarious Jew. He turned and ducked suddenly into a tiny doorway which seemed to shrink before his bulk. Then he was gone; I stood in the echoing nave while his singing spiralled slowly up into the tower.

After a while I made my way up the dark steps and found David posing for me in a recess, his legs crossed beneath him on the stone floor, his face turned towards the angled slit in the tower wall, a narrow meurtrière that gave onto the sea. The recess was no more than four or five feet wide at any point, and barely tall enough to stand up in. 'This is where she lived,' he said, and nodded at my look. 'Yup: a woman.' He nodded again, in solemn tribute.

'Just the one?' I said. 'I mean: no-one before or since?'

He shrugged. 'Could be, I don't know. She was the famous one. Maybe the only one. Would you want to live here for forty years? She was walled in, there was a wall right where you're standing. Just one little hole for food and water. Think about it.'

I didn't dare, it was too close to Edgar Allan Poe. A silence fell, the longest I'd ever experienced with David—and he was a connoisseur of silences. It started badly. Edgar Allan Poe: if David knew what I'd done, would he wall me up here, where nobody would hear my screams, was that why he'd brought me here, had he guessed, did he know? But gradually I pulled myself together, searching for something peaceful to concentrate on instead, gazing out of the tall, narrow slit in the wall, at the fading light and the sea.

Once a seagull crossed, drifting, wobbling on a stream of warmer air. A pause, then it returned. I waited for it to come back. Waiting, I converted it into a different bird, into the buzzard above Gwaun valley, Bromley's buzzard. The image persisted, as though I was willing it into view. But it wasn't the buzzard I was after, it was what the buzzard saw: the domed hilltops of tussocky grass, of mice and voles and running creatures, and in the valley below, trees and hedgerows, houses snug as nesting birds; the two worlds twinned, contained, reflected in the buzzard's eye.

Darkness gathered from the corners of the cell, cloaking David's figure.

'Said her prayers once or twice,' came his voice. 'Watched the sea. The windmill was maybe there already. Watched the fishing boats come in.' Another silence, as the wind got up and battered at the stone, swelling the sense of peace inside. 'Listened to the wind. Said her prayers once more.'

I shifted. David's face, barely distinguishable, turned to me. 'What do you think, Jackson?'

'I'd go mad.'

He looked back at the narrow window, at the unison of sky and sea. 'Would you?'

I said, 'You fancy it, do you?'

'Didn't you know? I've fixed it with the vicar, I start tomorrow, early.'

I laughed, and thought: *the day that I became a monk.* I decided I'd better tell David about the Bromley business before Sue did. She'd only make my behaviour sound ridiculous. There in the echoing cell I retold the story from the moment following the accident to Sindacombe's breakfast-time visit, stressing the similarities between the two men but without, I thought, overstating my case; without drawing conclusions. David drew his own.

'Brother Thurgo,' he said, 'you have been a great fool. Say one hundred Hail Marys and kiss my feet.'

Kiss his feet? 'Why have I been a fool?' I said.

'Didn't you know that God subsidizes the Devil?'

I stared at him in the darkness. I couldn't make out his face, much less his feet.

'I don't follow,' I said. There was a pause.

'What I said: didn't you know that God the Father subsidizes the Devil.'

'Does that mean you think it's Bromley all along? That it's one person?' I was utterly bemused.

'What does it matter?' came David's voice. 'You shouldn't be surprised when they wear the same face, that's all.'

'Sue doesn't believe it's Bromley,' I said, trying to force him into an answer.

'Saints and martyrs,' he said blithely, 'aren't permitted such knowledge. They'd never do the washing up. Now,' he stood up, blocking the last chink of light, 'begin your penance!'

'No thanks,' I said, and groped my way back down the stairs. I waited for him to follow, but he didn't. When I'd waited long enough, I called up, 'David?' What passed for Jewish oaths came faintly down the stairwell. After a while he spoke again: I was granted his blessing. Silence fell.

The swallows swooped at the sound of my footsteps as I crossed the nave, pulled back the heavy door, listened again. Silence. I let the door swing back and walked down to the cottage on my own.

FOR ONCE I was present at supper, but this time it was the master's place that lay empty, we were the tribe that laid an extra place. I told Sue that I had left David in the anchorite's cell.

'Oh ho,' she went, 'confessing his sins.' She and Claire shared a suppressed laugh; whatever they'd been discussing since we took our walk, it had cheered both of them up. 'That could take all night.'

Sue was in no mood to deal with Steffie, who had been fed while we were out, and put to bed. Over the meal Sue talked relentlessly about past jobs and opportunities David had always found a reason to decline. She mimicked him, to Claire's amusement. It was one meal I'd rather have missed, with its heavy gaiety. We ate David; but he too had prepared this feast and taken his share in the English manner, in absentia. After supper the women washed up, refusing help. When it was finished Claire went straight back upstairs. I watched her saunter gracefully out of the sitting room, and waited uneasily for Sue to join me. After a pause I heard her draw back a chair at the kitchen table and unclip her guitar case. She sat and began a mournful Stuart song, putting a series of fresh chords to it, repeating the first line in different keys over and over till my nerves were singing with her. As always in the sitting room I looked to the Rimbert street scene, on the wall, to site myself, tunnelling into a haven of slanting shadows, black and ochre like the twilit church nave, but peopled with homely figures poised to go about their business. Anxious, now, to go; Sue's riff recurred, maddening.

I stood and went to look in at the kitchen doorway. Sue watched her fingers, intent, on the guitar strings. I walked back and out of the hall; the Stuart song pursued me up the stairs, along the unlit corridor. At Claire's door I stopped a moment, thinking, and finally raised my hand to knock. 'Jack?' came her voice.

'Mm-hm.'

There was a pause. 'It's open.'

I entered. Claire was sitting on the carpet by the narrow bed, her back erect against the wall, her legs stretched out. I wondered for a moment whether she was doing exercises, but her face showed no sign of exertion; she eyed me impassively. I shut the door and glanced round. The room was small. A chest of drawers, a chair, a bed, perfectly tidy. An empty glass, a bedside clock; there were no other visible effects. Even the sketchbook and the paints were packed away somewhere. I almost laughed at the reproachful neatness, so unlike the rest of the cottage. The chair looked comfortable enough. A cosy corner in a pleasant room if Claire had wanted it that way, but no, I thought, the guardian of its anonymity sat on the floor, against the wall, keeping the tainted house at bay. I smiled. The artist's room: no wonder she produced still lives. Her answering smile told me that she had my number. Look at me, it said, look at my limbs, I'm not at war with this place, I'm elsewhere, snug, in space.

I took the armchair and we sat in silence, holding the smile. I was losing my bearings, watching her expression. It wasn't a knowing smile at all, I'd got that wrong too. No: friend or foe? was all it asked, in simple language. She looked down, releasing me. I tried to re-assess the room, and purge myself of my first, glib response. Begin again. But the walls offered nothing back, no images to ground my growing vertigo. Sue's fractured song came from below. Claire's blonde, bowed head, her parted hair, begged a caress. I forced my gaze away, around the room, searching, hoping for some attribute of her to redress the singlemindedness of my desire. What did she do, what did she look at, when she wasn't sketching; when she was alone here in her cell, what did she think about? I so wanted a way of liking her. There were no books, no photographs, no furry toys. No mirrors, unless these too were guiltily tucked away. Hardly; she seemed quite unburdened by her beauty—perhaps it was an object of sufficient meditation to replace all toys. I held on to this, it seemed to make a kind of sense; explained her body as an object alien to her. Like her paintings, like a toy, it seemed to have no moods; her own moods fluctuated independently. Her grace, her beauty, were no part of her, they were another place, a public monument which she maintained as neatly as she kept her room; as untouched by her thoughts. No wonder I felt vertigo before this chasm. I understood now why I had misinterpreted her earlier expression, when I came into the room. The smile had told me one thing, Claire herself another. But the vertigo was still there. Friend or foe? Before the girl looked up again I had to have an answer for her. The inner truth; the outward show. Could I be friends to both? Hands across the chasm? Yes—because it wasn't that when compared to her outward show the true Claire was a shallow thing, *banale*; on the contrary it was her beauty that was so *banale*, an alien surface, strange to her. That was the right way round: I could admire the inner Claire, and as for her beauty, hallelujah, that was perfectly *banale*. It merely happened to be perfect. Saints be praised.

160

Sue's singing had stopped. For good, I hoped. But Claire didn't look up at all, as minutes passed. We sat. I realized that she was waiting for me, not to talk: to move to her, or leave. I got up from the armchair and sat beside her on the floor. Claire offered no response, but it was easier than I'd expected; after all I'd already landed on that alien surface, her hand; already kissed her mouth. We'd had the words, the week before. But her peculiar beauty had no place for memory, it had been scrubbed, since, and was strange again. I felt a chill of hesitation; did I really want this? It would be like renting a building from the National Trust. I took her hand; no, it was warm, it clutched mine, and I felt happily ashamed of all my thoughts. The hand was moist, it answered with a more than corresponsive pressure, unlike Sue's measured responses which were doled out like an echo.

'Hot hands,' I said. She nodded. 'Sorry mine are so cold.'

She shrugged, and I bent down to her face. I saw it with a guilty pang. Her eyes were heavy with the threat of tears, and my nervous hostility dissolved.

'What is it?' But she wouldn't look at me. I squeezed her hand. 'Tell me.'

She shook her head. That sense of a perversely fabricated, too familiar but protective drama, settled on us for a moment. I was beginning to recognize it now, shadowing the wooing of a stranger. She had to shake her head and then I had to pause and say the next thing in a certain tone. It was there to be dispelled and rediscovered again like a flight path.

'Is it my fault?'

She shook her head again, faintly. Sue's voice came once more, drifting up outside the window, 'Here we come to Lady Queen Anne, vizzery vazzery vozzery rem...'

This time I was grateful for the serenade; it broke Claire's expression and she gave in with a smile. I touched her cheek and she didn't resist.

'At least it's a different one,' I said. Claire nodded. She tossed her hair back and pulled a hand firmly across her eyes. I let my hand fall.

'*Tizzery tazzery tozzery tem,*
  Hiram, Jiram, cockrem, spirem,
  Poplar, rollin, gem.'

'Have you ever been to hear her sing?' I said. 'In public?'

'Last year,' Claire nodded firmly; but her voice was still a little shaky.

'Perhaps they should form a duet, she and David, what with shooby-zoobs and vizzery-vozzery...'

Claire said nothing, looking up at the window. Her pressure on my hand remained the same. 'You've come to say goodbye?' she said, pulling her hair back with the other hand.

'Goodbye? No, I'm not going anywhere. What makes you think that?'

'Sue told me.'

'I'm in no hurry,' I said. She let go of my hand and wiped hers on her dress. *Hiram, Jiram,* came the lilting voice.

I wondered if David was listening too, from the tower. 'D'you think he's still in the priest's hole,' I grinned, 'at his penance?' David's earlier innuendo about himself and Claire came back in a rush, too late. I wished I hadn't spoken.

'I've been thinking about you a lot,' said Claire, and she looked down at my hand, still in her lap.

I couldn't move, or speak. All my moral contortions collapsed in a heap. I looked at her. She was still watching my hand, waiting. It was sin I was staring at now, homely and unadulterated; I was unprepared. Her words changed everything—it surely hadn't been like this for David, any more than between myself and Sue. I bent and kissed Claire on the cheek; I couldn't think; I moved to find her mouth. She pulled away against the side of the bed, and looked at me.

'That's all right,' I said. 'I feel a little ... carried away, myself.' I'd lost the flight path altogether. I put my hand against her shoulder. She didn't move back but her eyes turned stony, searching mine.

'Liar.' She gazed at me. I shook my head, and bent to prove it to her. But Claire was having none of it, and fought free. She turned against the bed and pulled herself to her feet. Her fingers were flicking and fidgeting with rage. She measured my gaze; it didn't calm her anger. She balled her fists, to stop them working. 'You're as bad as Sue ... you couldn't tell the truth if you tried.'

'But it is the truth,' I said. 'It's what I feel.' Her anger triggered mine. 'If you want some sort of cynicism, stick with David.'

'David?'

I nodded, staring into her eyes; I was going to force an answer. Claire took a breath and expelled it raggedly, trying to control her fury.

'What's he been telling you?' There was no hint of confession in her voice.

'Nothing specific.'

'I wouldn't go to bed with him if—' she caught herself up and stopped, as though hearing herself protest too much. But I didn't think she was lying, not about her actions at any rate.

She stood trembling, accusing both David and me with all her force, and yet in some mysterious way the chaste little room, and the smooth, taut limbs of the figure before me, remained unaffected, even by her rage. She was on fire, but her presence refused the message.

'That's what you think, is it?' she said fiercely.

'No,' I said. 'It isn't now. But I didn't know what to think.' I let myself back against the wall, taking her place. The house was silent now, around us. I looked away from Claire's rigid expression. I still hadn't come to terms with her earlier words, as heady as a declaration of love. What had I answered? that I felt a little carried away too—yes, that was all right, it was true—a little parsimonious even;

in fact, was it still my turn? Claire was standing waiting, I could sense it without looking, still stiff with outrage over David's imputations.

'He didn't say as much,' I said. 'He just sort of let me think so, that's all.'

'And you believed him!'

I turned to her. 'I'm sorry. Truly I am.' I could hear my tone changing, directing me. 'Can't you see? I was upset too.' The drama revived, I let it lead me. Claire's face was set, defiant. I was longing to comfort her, to say the words. I loved the disorder of her face. Her mouth wavered; she was fighting tears.

'Because I love you,' I said, appalled at myself. To my amazement nothing in me cried out to deny it. It was true; I loved her, her tears were my tears, the bare room was witness, all at once reproachless, right. No crowded frames, no spies to mock my words. I loved the lonely room, the empty stage awaiting us.

Claire's face was expressionless with conflict. I rose quickly, rushed to break the mask, I kissed her face, her eyes, her mouth. Her body moved in little spasms, out of time with mine, I was dizzy with tenderness, alight with the momentous aura of the words, filling the room. I drew back. Her body was still pressed against mine, but her eyes were sober.

'That's what I mean.' It was spoken in her dry manner, only a little blurred now with excitement; I made to speak but she shook her head, and her voice found its intended edge: 'You don't have to say things.'

I was determined to. But I saw her face turn hard again, and stopped myself. I had to offer something, I knew; something that sounded like the truth.

'I want you so much,' I said, and Sue's own words the night before came back to mock. I felt the room desert me.

Claire nodded twice, lightly. 'I know you do,' she said.

A faintly teasing manner had come, and softened her stare. But the room—the room had deserted me, not because I'd told the truth about wanting Claire but because I was lying. Oh I wanted her but at that moment more than wanting her I loved her with all my being and why, *why* wasn't I allowed to say so? She stood back from me. The front door sounded, downstairs, opening and shutting with a carefree noise. David's heavy tread moved under us, into the sitting room, and the sound faded. I cursed him for his timing.

Claire and I gazed at each other; no smile came to her face though she too was listening; I withheld mine. I couldn't read her eyes. She turned and walked to the bed, sat down, pensive, uninviting. My intoxication hung uselessly in my head, a separate self. I couldn't work out which I had betrayed, which I should serve. Claire offered no clues. She sat, motionless. Muffled noises came of logs falling beside the grate.

Her hands went up and she began to unbutton her dress. Calmly, ignoring me. I watched, uncomprehending, but unable to take my eyes off her slim shoulders, her delicate breasts as they came into view. The dress came off. She didn't look at me. This was too comical for words; was it my cue to leave, or to advance? Some sort of test? Or threat? The proud maiden shaming the Nazi beast: if *this* is what you want...? Claire slipped off her panties, her gaze crossing me once without examining my face, and pushed back the bedcover, naked. She climbed into bed and pulled the sheets up to her shoulders. And looked at me, expressionless.

Abruptly, a nasty suspicion crossed my mind. David downstairs; the sudden strip. Was there a hidden connection? Claire's words: I wouldn't go to bed with *him*, if... if; no matter what the if, there was unresolved emotion there. Was she giving herself to me to spite him? Well, I wasn't going to be a pawn in *that* game—

'You do look miserable.'

I glanced up, startled; there was laughter in the voice. 'Aren't you coming to bed?' said Claire.

Her smile was pleading, mocking, open. It spoke for her body, and her: both. I stared, all at sea again, but there was a haven of forgiveness in her eyes, it was so simple, she was telling me. She wanted me. The Dark Age of confusion lifted; I began to undress rapidly. Brethren, why is Brother Thurgo such a dolt? Why was I always rushing down the wrong corridor, to the wrong door? I had always thought I was the hero. Dolt! I was the fool. It was a great relief. Shivering, I hurried to the bed, and felt Claire's warm body against me, lithe and firm, as I snuggled down into the sheets.

IT WAS NOT an athletic night. I was too tired for a prolonged assault; and I don't think Claire wanted one either. It didn't seem to be her style. Or perhaps, having made the decision to entertain me physically on a more casual, friendly basis—was that it? I hoped it was—she found it harder to explore the complete repertoire of intimacy than Sue had. This was understandable enough; making love brought with it however involuntarily the echoes of our earlier declarations, and since there were no more tender words, this limited our adventurousness. What did take place was awkward but exciting; Claire was tense, long though I caressed her willing, boyish body. Unlike Sue she wrapped her arms around me, but in her different way she was just as silent as Sue was. I began to wonder whether Chrissie's greedy noises, wellnigh notorious in our building, weren't something of an exception.

Claire's remoteness, her lack of prompting other than her willingness, incited me, but largely to fantasies of what she might be doing while she lay instead, taut, a little fierce, willing me to satisfaction. Her body continued as the third party in our activity, neither acknowledging nor rejecting what I was doing with it, nor what its owner may have wanted it to do. I reached a climax—it was the fierce expression that excited me, so different from Sue's glad one—but it was less explosive, we had less history to celebrate, for one thing, and it was shadowed by the words that might be necessary in its wake. They weren't; not for Claire, at any rate. She had already ruled them out of court herself, and we lay in silence, more or less content. The sleep was the best part of it, tucked tenderly against her long slim back, holding her breasts. I was anxious for her, but I couldn't keep awake, and I didn't want to, for fear of finding that my anxiousness was for myself. I'd said I loved her; but it wasn't that that frightened me. I didn't love Claire and she knew it—I'd meant it at the time, and I consoled myself with that—but what sort of a husband would I make if I could so easily deceive myself, let alone Chrissie? An ordinary husband, no doubt. Self-deception would be obligatory. But it was quite beyond me to set out, cold-bloodedly, to be an ordinary husband; I didn't want to be a fool for life. What was it the hero was supposed to do? Search and feel guilty. I'd had enough of that. Claire lay motionless and breathing softly, easily, asleep or not. I couldn't see her face. I shut my eyes, with my face in her scentless hair, and drifted off into untroubled and unbroken sleep.

I woke up before her, and finding I couldn't doze, sat up. The room was bright, its cleanliness obtrusive in the morning light. A stiff breeze shook the windowpanes. I looked down at Claire. One childish arm projected from the sheets, along the blanket; she had never looked more desirable or more in unison with her body, but the same anxiety weighed on my heart, as if I hadn't slept at all. I slipped out of bed and dressed.

Shutting the door softly behind me, I could hear Steffie singing and playing in her room along the corridor. I went down the stairs and into the sitting room, where the smell of cigars lingered from last night. David's expensive smokes; what rows, or more likely what ruminations they bespoke, I didn't like to think. I walked through the kitchen with its windows glowing in the light, and out into the fresher, cooler garden. It occurred to me to take my buckled bicycle, waiting there for me like a trusty steed, and hobble to the station; but that would have been to compound my sense of crime. The full farewells were called for.

And as I stood there and surveyed the foliage, the breeze stippling the hedge with upturned leaves, the night and the distress began to drain from me. I had hoped for an immediate reprieve, on waking; but it came now. I recognized the same scoured-pot sensation of the morning before, alone in Sue's fourposter. I felt unaccountably well. Tested, whole. And tortoiseshelled, at last, against the worst. In two nights, I felt, I'd caught up a long way. I sunned myself, pacing the garden.

Claire's face appeared, briefly, behind her window, and withdrew. On the tower above the waving trees, the clock chimed out the quarter hours, harsh and new, and out of place; it would have deafened any anchorite. I tried my bicycle, and found the frame intact, the tubing straight. Upending it, I spun the wheels. The front one lolloped with a mocking warp, the rim rising and falling against my palm; I turned the frame upright and pushed it back again towards the tree, watching the tyre's eccentric orbit.

'Wotcher,' came a voice. Sue was gazing at me from her bedroom window, an unconvincing Cockney.

'Hi there,' I said.

'Going somewhere?'

'Not on this.' I rolled the lurching wheel. Sue leant back into the room, in conversation. Downstairs I could see Claire in the kitchen, busying.

'You want to come up?' Sue was at the window again. I nodded and, propping up my bike, made for the kitchen.

Efficient, unsmiling, Claire was loading a tray with David's delicacies. Raw egg, yoghourt, fruit. Fitness next to godliness.

'Breakfast in bed,' she said drily.

I came and kissed her on the cheek, taking her arm. She squeezed quickly back and moved off to the cooker. I perched on the table, watching her.

'Everything all right?' I said.

168

'I've got to get Steffie up, it's late.'

She hurried back with the coffee, and poured it, splashing some.

'You know that isn't what I meant.'

Claire took the saucepan to the sink. 'It was nice,' she said gently, without looking round.

It was too nice; I wanted my enigma back; anger, anything. She came back and picked up the tray. I blocked her path, unable to shake off the scene and let it pass. 'Aren't we going to say *any-thing*?'

Claire looked down at the tray. I followed her gaze; the gelatinous eye of the egg stared back at us. She shook her head.

'Fine,' I said. I let her through and followed her into the sitting room and up the stairs.

David waited like a pasha in the giant bed, and smiled at the arriving retinue, bare-chested, at ease, patting his stomach. He watched Claire. Sue watched me, amused.

'Thank you.' David adjusted the tray on his lap, and Claire retired, ignoring us. The door had hardly shut before he freed a coarse chuckle, eyeing me gleefully. I rode this with a straight face, getting no comfort from Sue, who walked smiling towards the tray. David slowly subsided. 'Hee hee...' he muttered, and poured egg into his mouth.

'Coffee?' said Sue.

I nodded. David eyed me sternly, wiping his beard.

'How now, donzel! Art mallicolly after tha co-ee-tus?'

'Shh!' went Sue. 'She's next door...'

'I don't give a shit. She fucked him, didn't she?'

Sue returned his stare. 'So? What are *you* so pleased about?'

'*Pleased?*' He lunged forwards off the pillows. 'Damn right I'm pleased.' I gestured urgently towards the wall behind him; but his eyes were on Sue.

'She's in Steffie's room,' I pleaded.

He rounded on me. 'What's the matter with *you?*' There was a silence as he sized me up, and leant back gloating. 'Okay, she was the worst piece of ass you've ever had. Right? That's too bad,' he said forgivingly, and began to scoop up his yoghourt like a starving bear. 'Little boy's ass, right?' he murmured into it. Then with his spoon raised, head on one side, he paused to consider this in a different light, and looked up at me, grinning. 'Zoobydooby.' He rattled the bed with a suggestive shake of the buttocks.

I knew none of this performance was intended for me. I glanced at Sue. It didn't help. She took her coffee to the door, ignoring both of us. 'I'll be downstairs,' she said. I moved towards her as she opened the door, but her expression stopped me. 'It's okay,' she said quietly, with a venomous look. 'I'll check the trains for you.' And she went.

David was devouring his food, abstracted, when I turned back. I heard Steffie's door open; Claire and the child followed Sue down the stairs. David glanced at me. 'Never mind, Jackson,' he pushed the tray back and slid luxuriously down under the flowered bedspread until only his bearded head showed above the sheet, gazed at the ceiling and hummed a few tuneless notes, 'the whirligig of time will bring in its revenges.' I walked to the window and perched on the sill, watching him.

'I thought you were getting up early today.'

He glanced at me, remembering. 'Special dispensation. They've never had a married anchorite before.' I shifted, anxious for a speedy farewell. 'Shut the window, will you?'

I did, relieved to have some task to perform. Yelps of delight from Stefanie rose from the kitchen. David buried his head in the pillow, pressing it around his ears.

'Well,' I said, but he was staring up, oblivious, not hearing me. His mouth was open, and the head, pouched in the pillow, looked unnervingly like John the Baptist's, sat in a pre-Raphaelite fourposter. After a time he turned his head towards the window, letting the pillow fall back against the bed.

170

'Well I guess I'll be seeing you in London,' he said. 'I'm sorry you're going.' I could see he meant it. He stared past me at the view, and paused. 'Things grow chillsome,' he said. '*Mais toujours gai*, Archie.'

LEAVING PROVED TO be fraught with difficulties. More fare-wells; struggling to wedge the bike into the boot of the Triumph—Sue had made up her mind to escort me, though I dreaded it—then finding the string to attach the yawning lid of the boot. And finally detaching Steffie, who wouldn't let me go, and danced chanting round the car while Sue shouted at her from the driver's seat, to clear the road.

As before, Claire's manner was muted, friendly, bidding a formal goodbye in the kitchen. Steffie covered our awkwardness with an impression of an anxious adult hostess, insisting I come again. I went out to the car, with the string the child had found for me, still piqued by the inconclusiveness. 'Salud,' said David solemnly, from an upper window. Sue was already waiting in the car, poised for a racing start. An idea came to me; I put down the string and returned to the kitchen.

Steffie looked up delightedly; Claire barely glanced, serene. I watched her tidy up her charge's breakfast place.

'Could I have one of your sketches?' I asked.

She paused, looking up at me. 'If you like.'

'Choose one for me.'

She shrugged, and smiled. 'You do it.'

'Please,' I insisted. But she was adamant.

'Take any one you like,' she said, 'they're not particularly precious.'

Steffie broke the silence. 'I'll choose!' she cried, and slid off her chair. She ran to the doorway and stopped, smirking. 'Can I get down?'

Claire nodded. 'They're under the bed,' she said, unsmiling.

I followed Steffie upstairs into the little room. The bed was already made, the impersonality complete. Steffie dived and emerged again from behind the counterpane, bringing the sketchbook. We leafed through it, on the floor. A depopulated Norfolk, moonscapes, met our gaze.

'That one!' Steffie pointed, firmly. The painting showed her own, gaudier contribution; it was one of their co-operative efforts.

'No, it's yours,' I said, and she stared sulkily at it, refusing to turn the page. 'Okay then; thank you,' I said and tore it out carefully. I was fed up with brooding monochromes, with my fruitless, selfish attempt to give our parting some colour.

'That's not all,' said Steffie. 'I want to give you something else. I know. Have tortoise.'

'No, I don't want tortoise.'

'We've all got to give you something, have we,' came a voice from the doorway, 'to get rid of you?' David stood grinning in a baggy pair of underpants, like an old-time prize-fighter.

'No,' I said, 'you've given me quite enough.'

His smile broadened to include a glance at Claire's bed. 'If you say so, Jackson.' Then he put on his grave expression. 'A word in your ear . . .' and he padded on towards the bathroom without waiting.

When I caught up with him, he was pissing attentively into the toilet bowl.

'How d'you find Sue?' he said.

I froze.

'Don't be shy. You must have talked.' He paused. 'Well? Should I give her one?' He turned to me, shaking an organ surrounded by greying hairs. 'Should I give her a baby, Jackson?' As I searched for an answer David tucked himself into his trunks, noting my expression, and perhaps mistook relief for a different emotion. 'You want to give her one?' he grinned.

I shook my head. He put an arm round me; pals. We stood for some time as if waiting for the photographer, David gazing meditatively at his naked feet.

'Write me your considered advice,' he said.

I squeezed his shoulder and slowly detached myself.

Outside, Sue was working at my bicycle, testing the web of string. She beckoned me wordlessly and we climbed into the car, with Steffie close behind us, dancing.

'*Ene mene mona mi,*

   Pasca lara bona bi...'

It sounded like one of Sue's own songs. She peered in at the window, as Sue waved her away. Steffie giggled, circling the car.

'*Elke, belke, bon!*' And it started all over again, *eeny meeny*, as though she knew just what had been going on. It was as well to be leaving now. When Steffie was rounding the back of the car, Sue let in the clutch and we shot forwards down the Green.

'That was clever,' began Sue bitterly, as we took the first corner; I knew she wasn't referring to Stefanie. But I'd had my fill.

'Who's talking?' I said. We drove through the town, in silence.

The coast road was crowded. Tourists lined the beaches; heads bobbed in the calm sea. We passed the site of my tumble from the bike on my way back from Cromer, and I turned and gazed anxiously at the jolting boot. Sue ignored me, lips set. I felt I had to break the mood, if only to reach the station without incident.

'Oh, don't be angry,' I said. 'Please...'

'It's safe,' she said curtly without looking round at the bicycle, 'I saw to it myself.'

A queue of cars kept us from Sheringham, and the waiting finally broke her pent-up reserve. She gave up the thought of pulling out to overtake and sat back, hands dropping from the wheel. Stretching, she mussed her heavy hair back.

'Why did you have to do it *now?*' she said. 'Why did you have to do it now, when he came back?'

'You mean *that's* not right, but—'

Her eyes held mine, fiercely. 'You don't understand anything, do you?'

We moved a little way forwards to catch up with the car in front. I saw myself missing my train, and began to fidget.

'She'll have to go now, that's all,' said Sue, dragging on the handbrake. I turned to her, astonished and ready to burst out angrily. 'No,' she said, watching me, 'you don't see, do you. You were right there and you couldn't see it. He'll be chasing her all round the house when I get back.'

I shook my head. 'Talk about double standards.'

'No, damn you!' It was almost a shout, and I half expected the driver in front to turn around. 'I told you before, I don't give a snap what he does as long as I don't get it over dinner. Why the hell did you have to do it last night?'

'I'm sorry,' I said. 'I mean, wouldn't he be chasing her anyway?'

She was looking away. The traffic was moving forwards. 'Thanks,' she said. We edged through Sheringham in silence. I longed to make amends, but couldn't find the words for it. Incurious shoppers threaded their way round us, busy and indifferent as the figures in the painting on the sitting room wall. I'd forgotten to say goodbye to it.

I wondered about Sue's sense of outrage. Hadn't she pushed me and Claire together, even last night? And the stumbling adolescent opera that followed, wasn't it partly their creation, Sue's and David's both—I wondered whether Claire had felt this too—right down to the dialogue, their presence in and out of the words?

The little halt was empty when we pulled up beside it. No train, no-one waiting. My heart sank.

'It's all right,' said Sue, sitting back and switching off the engine. She glanced at her watch. 'I gave us plenty of time.'

I took her arm, but she ignored it, unforgiving, and opened the car door to get out.

Together, at the boot, we undid the string and lifted out the awkward arms of metal. A bicycle took shape out of it again as I stood it on the shiny, melting tarmac. I pushed it towards the platform steps, hoping Sue would follow, and heard her footsteps behind me as I lifted the machine to carry it up. The platform shimmered in the heat, bare, a featureless wire fence along its length; not even a sign giving the station's name. There was a bench, and I put the bicycle against the fence beside it. The silent rails stretched out beside old, dismantled yards, half a mile of empty track into a distant curve. Sue sat down on the bench and closed her eyes, the sunlight turning the edges of her thick, dark hair to bronze. Her full features seemed whitened, masklike in the glare. I sat beside her, to speak.

'You said... all you wanted was a friend. I'd like to try. In spite of everything.'

She opened her eyes, staring ahead, sybilline.

'It's not my fault,' I went on, 'what's happening between you and David.'

Sue nodded faintly, passive, lazy in the sun.

'Look...' she sighed, and brought one large hand up to shade her eyes, 'don't be like him. David doesn't know what he wants, he busts through people's lives...' She shook her head, letting her hand drop, and turned back to the sun, expressionless. 'Find what you want and settle for it. Maybe then we can be friends.'

I watched her in silence. She glanced at me, then back again, at rest. 'What are you thinking?' she said.

'Just thinking.' I wiped my head, my hair.

'The other night... that was okay, wasn't it?' A more vulnerable tone had come into her voice. I nodded, studying her. 'We'd already made it years ago, really. Hadn't we?'

Yes; all that talking, and touching, over the years. I suppose. Did that mean we hadn't sinned, didn't have to repent? Sue turned, after a pause, to search my face. 'Say something,' she said.

I squeezed her hand. The words weren't coming. She mistook my squeeze for sympathy. 'We'll be all right,' she said, 'the old buffalo and I, we'll be all right.'

I nodded again and glanced down the empty track. 'I'd like to settle down,' I said.

'Oh sure,' said Sue, 'I know what *you* want, but it's the old story, you don't want what goes with it.'

Without sound, without seeming to move towards us, the train had appeared on the distant curve. I looked down, relieved.

Sue made a little noise, beside me. 'Hnh?' she repeated, trying to tease me out. I smiled. 'Okay,' she shrugged, as if dismissing her own scepticism. 'But just make sure it's what you really want. Remember what the lady said. All dreams are prophetic. *All* dreams.'

With a soft hiss of brakes, the train came slowly past the bench, and halted.

AT LIVERPOOL STREET station I was still undecided as to whether I should head for Highgate and deposit the bike or go straight to Hammersmith on it, hoping the long ride wouldn't prove too dangerous on a bent wheel. The thought of Chrissie's letters, or the hope of them, won; with Claire and Steffie's sketch wrapped up inside it I strapped my jacket to the saddlebags and wobbled out into the traffic. The one way system at the Angel and, later, Hammersmith nearly saw the end of me, but I survived to reach the relative quiet of King Street and its plane trees, ignoring streetside comments on my jerky action.

I let myself into the house and sorted frantically through the communal mail at the foot of the stairs. Beneath the bills and travel brochures lay an airmail letter with my name, address, and Chrissie's familiar italic flourishes. I stuffed it into my trouser pocket and searched for more, but it was the only one from her; I fetched my jacket and the saddlebags, and bounded up the flights of stairs to the flat.

'*Darling Jack*—' I skipped the narrow leaves of paper, tourist anecdotes and Florentine discoveries, to the last page, the last paragraph, where the endearments clustered. *Dearest, darling, only love*; I leant back against the door, read and reread them greedily, reassured that the letter could carry no unwelcome shocks, with such an ending, studded with delicious innuendoes, promises. I found my way to our kitchen and sat on the table, dazed.

In time I read the letter from the top, evoking Chrissie's flock of marauding tourists, all their best comments stored and reproduced for me, in turn; the innocent wonderment of David's less world-weary compatriots. Again I lingered over the tantalizing close.

The sunlight poured into the little kitchen. Dust lined the cluttered worktops and the fridge; our posters sagged, askew, victims of our upstairs neighbours and their parties. I gazed at the familiar disarray, at cans and pans and plates. Lunchtime; but I wasn't hungry. I stood and fetched some paper, paused, decided on the bedroom, and picked out a book to press on. I pushed myself back on the bed, against the wall, and contemplated the blank sheet. I began.

'*My darling—I've just got in and found your letter. Read all the dirty bits first. Too excited to eat—I'm sitting down to this right away. Sorry I haven't written, I've been in Norfolk, at Sue's cottage. Much to tell! I meant to write but got caught up in a strange business with an old master of mine from The Arbor days called Bromley, I must have mentioned him. He was in a car crash and I identified him. He's retired now and presumably, I thought, on holiday. Then things got complicated—the police said he was someone else. I tracked him down, Bromley this is, and he seemed thoroughly suspicious. Up to something shady obviously. Also the other man was out of hospital by this time. But nobody believes me! Certainly not Sue—you can imagine why. She and David are in worse disarray than usual.*'

I stared at the page, already sickened by its tone. I slowly crumpled it up, and sat; it was some time before I began again, and when I wrote it was amid lengthening pauses.

'*My darling—sorry I haven't written for a week or more. I've just got in. I've been all over the place, travelling non-stop—to see my mother (witch-hunting in Cornwall), David and Sue, even an old schoolmaster from The Arbor days whom I confused for someone else, in Norfolk. Sounds crazy I know, but it gives you some idea how distracted I've been. Thinking so much about you—and about us. I want to try and put some of it into words, which won't be easy. And it's probably a cowardly way to do it, but at least it gives you time to think about it.*

'*You've probably been thinking the same thoughts, at some stage or another, I don't know. To come to the point: I'm not sure we can go on like this, indefinitely. Or rather I'm not sure whether I can. I've had one or two adventures along the way, this summer, which have made me think. About myself, that is—I've never doubted your loyalty (laugh if you like). It's not simply a matter of physical loyalty, anyway, is it? But if I can't trust myself without you, then I feel I'm not going to be offering enough of myself to you—even in the short term. I've thought about this and I wonder whether we shouldn't stay apart for a time. It's probably a'*

I found myself trembling, and stopped. I read it through but I wasn't taking in the words. I sat for a long time again, until the trembling stopped, and then put the book and paper aside and went into the kitchen. I opened some soup and heated it up, staring into space. I couldn't get the letter I'd been writing into focus. The sentences became less and less clear. I walked back towards the bedroom, slowly, and stood in the doorway. The paper, with my crowded writing, lay on the bed; but I stayed where I was, gazing at the shape of it, the trail of ink.

When I came back into the kitchen, the soup was bubbling, a brown, angry bog. I poured it into a mug and blew on it, listening to the sounds from the street, my mind a willing blank. The soup tasted of nothing at first, then gradually warmed me; I added pepper and began to savour it. I sat, enjoying every mouthful. Homely oxtail, but I drained the last lumpy streak regretfully. I washed out the mug along with several week-old dishes and put them away. I went round the room and put each poster straight in turn, standing back, adjudging them.

I marched back to the bedroom; and knew what I was going to do. I sat back on the bed and snuggled into the corner. I placed the previous draft on the bedside table, and lifted my pen to start a new page.

'Darling Chrissie—I want you to marry me.'

I stared at it. I'd meant it, I told myself, as an experiment; to see the way it looked on the page. But I couldn't see the words. Perhaps they were the wrong ones for the purpose. I put the sheet aside.

'Darling Chrissie—will you marry me?'

It looked better, and also foolish. I put it by the other sheets, and lay back, dizzy. I shut my eyes to try and rest. I couldn't; the peppered oxtail worked, within. This was absurd. I sat up and made a pile of the different drafts, put them on the bedside table, and went out to fetch the saddlebags.

I brought them back and unpacked hurriedly, strewing my laundry on the floor. A bulky object came to hand as I opened the second saddlebag. It was wrapped in tissue paper. I drew it out, puzzled: a frame. Taking off the paper, I saw it was the Rimbert painting. Emotions came, too many, spilling over for the first time.

As I tried to take in the familiar figures I realized I was crying. I lay on the bed, now free of letters, with the painting on my chest, and let the tears come.

When I sat up and slowly came to unpack further, I found a note, unsigned, but clearly packed by Sue along with the gift. It was a handwritten page, in Sue's writing, a passage framed in quote-marks but unattributed.

'Like meaning itself, light does not reside in the scene depicted—it crosses the frame, always from left to right, out of a leaded window so narrowly profiled that we glimpse neither a landscape nor the source of light. In Vermeer the beyond has no features. Yet in our world, in the man-made world of the room illuminated by this transitory light, hangs a map...'

I read on, blindly, in love with the calm flow of the words, and set it down finally on the bedside table, covering my stumbling letters with its serene authority.

I didn't want to hang the picture yet. I left it, on the bed, a darker room within the room, and took the empty saddlebags down the hallway and out into the street, through a narrower door, onto a harsher, brighter pavement. I needed the air, the movement, and I took the bicycle on its last lap, to Highgate, where I could bring it a new wheel, in time.

The long climbs, steadying the bike, took all my mind, and I was grateful for it, and almost sorry to reach my mother's house. I peered in through the basement windows as I pushed the bike towards the coal-hole where it lived, but I could see no sign of Molly.

Coming back up the steps towards the street, I found the landlord, Geoffrey, standing in the open door, watching me. He was a tall, cadaverous-looking man, prissy in his tone yet smelling muskily of pipe tobacco and usually sporting one of my mother's home-made cardigans, with shag in both pockets.

'Just missed her,' he said gloomily. 'Got hold of you at last, then.'

In the road a pneumatic drill had begun to chatter.

'I'm sorry?'

'I say she's got hold of you at last, then. Your mother.'

'No,' I said. 'Why? Has she been trying?'

'Trying?' he exclaimed, and shook his head in wonderment. 'She's been desperate.' He paused. 'You haven't heard, then.'

I stared at him. He seemed to be relishing the moment.

'Your father's turned up,' said Geoffrey, with a small smile. The drill sounded, in the road, away behind us, stuttering, hammering at the pavement. *B-B-B-Bromley drill.* It paused.

'No,' I said patiently. 'You've got it wrong, Geoffrey.' He took pleasure, it had often struck me, in these teasing detours and confusions of his.

'I haven't got it wrong,' he said, giving me a fastidious look. 'Your father. Molly bumped into him at Selfridges. No, wait . . . it wasn't Selfridges. *One* of those places. Bourne and Hollingsworth. In the cafeteria, anyway. Taking lunch at Bourne and Hollingsworth.' The drill pounded for several moments and we waited, staring.

Shut the door, boy! Were you b-b-b-b-

'I think Molly wants to see you rather urgently,' he said as silence returned.

B-b-born in a cave?! Bourne and Hollingsworth? I couldn't take it in at all. 'My father?'

'Yes.' The pneumatic engine pumped again, briefly. 'I didn't know you had one, actually,' said Geoffrey vaguely.

I waited for the drill. It didn't come. I couldn't speak.

To Liskeard, *of which* Cley *is the first volume, con-tinues with* Richard's Feet, *published by Heinemann and currently available in a Minerva paperback edition. As in the two books to follow, a new narrator recounts the separate adventures that bring him or her nearer with each tale, and each book, to a reunion with the others in the Cornish town of Liskeard.* In Richard's Feet *the story-teller is a gigantic gargoyle of a man who for twenty years has been masquerading as an ex-Nazi in Hamburg: Richard Thurgo, of Cornish and Irish blood, once a London solicitor and now one of the kings of the Reeperbahn—'The World's Most Sinful Mile'.*